HIS FORBIDDEN LOVE

MANHATTAN BILLIONAIRES

AVA RYAN

1

MICHAEL

"THIS IS BULLSHIT."

I reluctantly turn my attention away from my ongoing perusal of the women in this black-tie crowd—still no sign of her, to my intense displeasure—and frown.

"Come again?"

"This. Is. Bullshit." Jake Quinn, one of my longtime best pals from freshman year at NYU umpteen years ago, scowls. "Remind me. Why am I here?"

This idiot.

"I told you," I say, not bothering to hide my impatience. "We're celebrating the retirement of one of my mentors. Dr. Smith. We're enjoying his lovely dinner cruise along the scenic Hudson River." I lean a hip against the railing and gesture at Lady Liberty with my drink hand (scotch and soda) and then downtown Manhattan with my free hand. It's a balmy June night, not too humid, and my hopes are high despite my best efforts to keep them in check. Nothing else conveys glamour, excitement and limitless possibilities like the glittering skyline stretching in front of us. With the jazzy music, strong drinks and tasty hors d'oeuvres, this little shindig has the makings of a decent event. Good things happen on nights like this. Hopefully tonight will be no exception. "Don't you want to wish a fellow doc well in the next chapter of his life?"

"Not particularly. I don't even know the guy. You're the plastic surgeon here. Not me."

"I need moral support, and you were the only one available. Which means that you're my plus-one," I say. "Congratulations."

"Yeah, well, I'm not fucking you at the end of the night. Just so you know."

I choke back a laugh. "Noted."

"Where the hell is Liam tonight?" he continues sourly. "Why didn't *he* get the honor?"

"Holed up at home with my sister, I'm assuming. Living his best life."

The third member of our college crew, Liam Wilder, recently reconciled with my twin sister Mia, who also attended NYU. The two of them had a nasty breakup after graduation but now seem to be on their way to a happy ending after all those years apart. Thank God. I'm close to both and maintaining my neutrality this whole time has not been easy.

"Lucky bastard. I should be home, too," Jake says, checking his watch for the umpteenth time. "I'm not sure the sitter can handle my kids."

I somehow manage not to roll my eyes. Life has been tough for Jake ever since he and his wife split a couple of years ago, leaving him a single dad with two small children. I get that. What I don't get? His persistent refusal to make things easier on himself and get full-time help.

"I keep telling you, for the love of God and the sake of my sanity, hire a nanny. You need one now more than ever."

Jake, Liam and I are all physicians. In addition to our full-time practices, we recently sold a medical device that Liam invented (Jake and I were initial investors) for a shit-ton of money. If you've come up with a number, throw a few more zeros behind it and you'll start to get the picture. We're all suddenly rich beyond our wildest dreams, which means we've got a lot more money for luxury living. None of us has plans to head to Barbados and bask in the sun for the rest of our lives, though. We all enjoy what we do and work insane hours. Hence Jake's need for a nanny.

Jake grimaces, sips his drink and does his best to avoid my gaze.

"This isn't about *me*," he says. "Why do *you* need moral support? You're a grown man."

I hesitate because he's right. It sounds way too overblown to tell him the truth, which is that I'm still inexplicably fixated on a resident I trained four years ago —and who's hopefully somewhere in the crowd tonight.

But the thing is, I'm divorced now, and...

And nothing. I don't know what I'm thinking, exactly. Can't even roll it into a ball of an idea to toss around. The time isn't right for me to be engaging in, I don't know, *stuff*. The ink is barely dry on my divorce. Said divorce was my fault because I proposed to my ex-wife despite my whispering doubts (we met at the gym and, while smart and beautiful, Patricia possesses all the warmth of Saturn's outer rings and always resented my commitment to my career) and then took five years to reverse the mistake. I went so far as to follow her to L.A. when she got a killer tech job, and only came back to NYC recently. So the wreckage of my personal life is still scorched, smoldering and throwing off occasional sparks. Plus, I'm in the middle of counting my new money and launching my new plastic surgery practice group back at my original hospital. I don't have the time or inclination for anything other than the occasional hookups everyone needs to take the edge off his or her basic needs.

The bottom line?

There's no logical reason why this woman is still on my mind. No explanation I can produce.

But she is.

Maybe *that's* why I'm here. To see her again and prove to myself that she's not the mythical and irresistible creature I've made her out to be in my mind. She can't be. I've blown her up in my mind. You know the phenomenon. It's like when you have a great dinner at a restaurant and can't wait to go back to enjoy it again, only to discover, say, that it was saltier than you remember or that the restaurant has changed hands and the new chef doesn't know what the hell he's doing with a frying pan.

Disappointment is inevitable. But I need to know.

"There's this, ah, woman," I say, uncomfortably aware of Jake's sharpening interest. I hastily down the rest of my drink, mostly to give myself something to do.

"And…?"

I try to look politely puzzled by the question.

"I think she'll be here."

Correction: I *know* she'll be here because a) she also worked closely with Dr. Retirement during her intern year; and b) I scoped out her nametag on the reception table when we checked in for tonight's cruise.

Dr. Ally Harlow.

I may as well confess that my surveillance efforts went a bit beyond nametag research. For example, the inter-webs revealed that she's now a plastic surgeon, like me, and will soon be done with her residency. I also now know that, unfortunately, she keeps her social media private. Which means that I *don't* know whether she's married with two and a half kids or not. A possibility that feels as though it would ruin a lot more than just my evening.

Jake's expression slides into amused incredulity, making my cheeks burn hotter than they already are.

"Pro tip: call her," he says. "She probably has a phone."

Like it's that easy for me to cold-call her after all this time. Like I've got an outgoing or engaging personality with people I don't know well. Please. My residents called me the Sphinx behind my back. They also used other, much more colorful descriptions, none of which I want to repeat here. My ex-wife once told me, and this is an actual quote, that attempts to communicate with me are like "watching a hostage video and trying to read between the lines."

So you understand my dilemma and why I need moral support. I'm no charmer.

"You know I'm not good with people," I say, exasperated. "Stop acting brand-new."

"Well, *that's* sadly true."

"Pretend you're a good wingman and—"

I catch sight of a woman walking through the crowd and stop dead, my heartbeat stumbling and stopping like a bike-riding kid who hits the curb and flips over the handlebars. She wears a coppery dress and has sports-toned legs, a deliciously curvy ass and a telltale tumble of sandy curls.

"Breathe," Jake says wryly, clapping a hand on my shoulder for a supportive squeeze. "You don't want to swallow your tongue."

Now he tells me.

I keep one eye on her as I thrust my empty glass at Jake. I know I have a decent chance of tracking her down again unless she suddenly jumps overboard and swims for the shore. But I still don't want to let her out of my sight.

"Be right back."

"Go get 'em, tiger," Jake calls after me, chuckling.

I weave my way through the crowd. The throng of people is endless, as though they're all pouring out of a clown car hidden nearby and determined to block me. By the time I catch up to her, she's settled at an out-of-the-way spot at the back of the boat, her elbows resting on the railing as she enjoys the view. The breeze sifts through her hair and carries her scent right to my nose. It's something warm and inviting, with a hint of vanilla. Something that doesn't help my equilibrium. At all.

By now, I've had a minute to gather my thoughts and cobble a few words together. I'm George Clooney or Will Smith in my mind, casual and charming for once as I slide in next to her and mirror her posture with my arms on the railing.

Great to see you, Ally.

Is that you, Ally? I'd hoped I'd see you here.

Something like that.

Don't screw this up, Jamison, I warn myself, and for one euphoric second, I feel like I won't.

So it's with grave internal disappointment that I open my mouth and bark the following in the exact same tone with which I used to order her to get a complete blood count on a patient:

"Harlow. Thought that was you."

She stiffens, her breath catching. It takes her a beat or two for her to turn her head and look at me, a delay long enough to give me the crazy idea that she recognizes my voice, that she needs to collect herself before facing me. Then her eyes meet mine, and I feel the connection as a pulse of electricity that makes all the fine hairs on my body stand on end before shooting up my nape and out through the top of my head. Swear to God, it feels powerful enough to light the entire island of Manhattan from Harlem to the Financial District the next time we have a blackout.

"Dr. Jamison. Hi."

It's hard to notice and catalogue every single detail about a person during a two-second increment of time, but I manage it like a pro as I stand there watching her. The clear, musical quality of her voice, exactly the way I remembered it. Those big, whiskey-colored eyes, a bit older and wiser now. That honeyed skin. The way her wide cheekbones taper to a pointy chin, giving her a heart-shaped face. The perfect cupid's bow atop those lush lips. And that *hair*. There's a Disney movie—*Brave*, I think —where the heroine's red hair does its own thing. Almost as though it's a living being with a pulse and a personality. Ally's hair is like that, only it's the perfect marriage of light brown, blond and this golden color that makes me think of unfiltered sunlight. It curls. It spirals. It falls on either side of her face and swings past her shoulders. It flutters with the breeze. It features prominently in my fantasies of her, where I fist it in my hands as it trails over my belly. Fantasies that have been plentiful since the second I laid eyes on her and which, as you can imagine, were damn inconvenient back when I was married.

Anyway, *she* said something. Now *I* should say something. That's how it works.

I open my mouth. Nothing comes. Probably because I'm grappling with a tinge of despair in realizing I didn't imagine or exaggerate anything about her. The unmistakable warmth is still there in her bright eyes. The musical quality in her voice is still there. If anything, she's *more* than she was before, the human equivalent of a finely aged bottle of wine.

I'm not sure that's good news for me.

I'm not sure at all.

"I was wondering if you'd be here," she says.

This information feels like a lotto win.

Tell her you were hoping she'd be here, whispers the voice inside my head, a smarter version of myself whose advice I don't follow often enough.

"Yeah?" I say instead, trapped inside my reserved personality like a rat in a cage.

"Yeah. I know Dr. Smith was your chief resident when you were an intern." She hesitates. "And I'd heard you were back from Los Angeles."

Fun fact: Ally and I last saw each other at a bar near the hospital one night at the end of my year as chief resident and her year as my intern. After which *I* headed to UCLA for my fellowship and *she* took a brief leave of absence. I wasn't big on moving out west, but Patricia got that job, and, like I said, I wanted to save my marriage if I could. God knew she'd sacrificed enough for me and my medical career. God also knew that I needed to leave the hospital, because saving my marriage and fighting my attraction to Ally while working with her at the hospital every day were mutually exclusive. Unfortunately, it turns out that geographical changes don't save failing marriages. Something I wish someone had told me sooner.

The upshot? I packed up my shit and booked a flight back to NYC as soon as Patricia and I finalized our divorce.

Now here we are.

"I'm back," I say. "Were they appropriately abusive to you residents after I left?"

"They were," she says with a dramatic shudder. "It was torture. I still have the scars."

"Good."

She grins, activating her dimples and flashing her white teeth. The effect is dazzling, like the lights coming up on stage at the beginning of a Beyoncé concert, and the butterflies swooping through my gut like fighter jets react accordingly.

I ease closer, drawn to that smile. To her.

"They weren't up to *your* standards, though," she adds.

This information pleases me greatly.

"Few are. So what are you doing now?"

"Studying for my boards," she says ruefully. "Trying to land a fellowship in plastics."

"Here?"

She pauses, a shadow hovering over her expression just as a gust of wind whips up her hair. The silken strands tickle their way down my cheek and across my lips. Not exactly the sight of her dropping to her knees in front of me, but the effect is similar in terms of winding me up. I pull the thick curls away from my face and take my sweet time letting them slide free. And if a deft move or two wraps the strands around my fingers in the process (I'm a surgeon; I've got good hands), that's not the end of the world, is it?

I certainly don't think so.

Neither does she, judging by her rising color and sudden breathlessness as she gathers all that glorious hair and tosses it over her shoulder.

"Sorry," she says, her voice a little husky now. "I can't control what my hair does on any given day. Didn't mean to assault you."

Assault away, angel.

It's okay, I want to tell her, but my fingers tingle and I need to figure out whether I'm imagining the way she's looking at me with those glittering eyes. Whether the glitter comes from the city's skyline or the kind of sexual attraction that I feel for her.

I could use a pep talk from my reluctant wingman right about now, but I know what he'd say. *Ask her out, moron.*

So I open my mouth, determined to go for it.

"Listen," I begin, my voice gruff. "Do you want to —"

"Here's your drink, babe," comes an unwelcome new voice, breaking the spell between us and making me tense up.

A male voice.

I manage to look around without giving him the evil eye, a difficult feat with jealousy suddenly clamped around my throat. And there he is, wrapping a proprietary arm around her waist and kissing the cheek that I would dearly love to kiss. Her date. Or worse.

But…no.

A glance at her hand as she accepts a glass of champagne reveals no rings.

I breathe easier. Not much, but some. They're not married or engaged. Hopefully, she just met this guy a few weeks ago and plans to dump him for his use of a lame–ass endearment like *babe*. I wait for the introductions with what seems like my entire existence hanging in the balance.

"Thanks," she tells the guy, looking flustered as she gestures at me without meeting my eye again. "This is, ah, Dr. Michael Jamison. My chief resident when I was an intern."

I can't manage a credible *good to meet you*. "How're you doing?" I say instead, extending my hand.

I take a good look at him as he switches his beer to the other hand and we shake. That's when I get another shock.

He doesn't *quite* hit my height of six-two, but he's fit like me. I'm guessing he's in his thirties, like me. He has tan skin, dark hair and a close-cropped beard. Like me. We could be brothers. If they ever make a movie about my life, central casting will send over *this* guy.

"Bruce Whitaker," he says as I'm still trying to absorb what I'm seeing. He doesn't have my deep voice, but it's damn close. "Ally's boyfriend."

2

ALLY

WHAT WERE you about to ask me? I desperately want to ask Dr. Jamison, but the moment and the question have slipped away with Bruce's arrival. Funny how his appearance when I'm talking with Dr. Jamison feels as though I've crossed the black and white wires while replacing a light fixture in my apartment and given myself a nasty shock. Some things aren't meant to touch. It feels strange to see two important men from different periods in my life together in the same space. The man I wanted when I was a lovesick intern versus the man I'm with now.

But here we all are.

My manners kick in and I perform the social niceties. I watch it all unfold with the muted horror with which I once watched Ripley announce her plans to go back and rescue Newt in *Aliens*: the introduction of my boyfriend of six months to the married man with whom I was once so obsessed that I lapsed into a major depression and needed to take a leave of absence from my residency, which almost ruined my medical career.

It's really unbelievable.

Ten seconds in Dr. Jamison's presence and I'm right back to where I always was with him, badly shaken, buzzing with adrenaline and high from the fresh cedar scent of his cologne. He affects me *that* strongly.

I can't fight the feeling that I'm seriously screwed here. It's all I can do to repress a burble of hysterical laughter.

This whole situation is my own fault. I knew there was a possibility that Dr. Jamison (yes, I still call him Dr. Jamison or the Sphinx, even in the privacy of my own thoughts; old habits die hard) would show up tonight. I knew things could get awkward, in my head if nothing else. But Bruce lives in D.C., and this was his weekend to visit me here in the city. So what was I supposed to do? Ask him to sit home alone while I enjoy an elegant black-tie evening without him? That doesn't seem like the sort of thing to strengthen our growing relationship.

Neither does discovering that I'm still wildly attracted to Dr. Jamison after all this time and that I'm still susceptible to flights of fancy about the way he may or may not be looking at me, for that matter.

Neither does realizing — I mean really *realizing*, for the first time ever — that Bruce looks like Dr. Jamison.

It's one thing to swipe on Bruce's profile on my dating app and think, *Huh, yeah, tall, dark and handsome — maybe I have a type*, and something else entirely to see the two men standing together as though they're gauzy mirror images of each other.

And don't get me started on the fact that my perfectly lovely Bruce now seems like a pale imitation of something I didn't even know I was trying to copy. It's like uprooting the reproduction of the Eiffel Tower from the Vegas Strip and planting it next to the original in Paris. Nothing like a side-by-side comparison to make you realize that, while the general effect is right, the two things aren't the same.

They're not the same at all.

Bruce? He's handsome, sure, but he doesn't possess Dr. Jamison's quiet authority that allows him to command every room he walks into. Bruce's brown eyes are kind and warm, not a piercing aquamarine that overflows with latent intensity. If someone wanted to give Bruce a nickname based on some mythological creature, I'm quite sure it would be something cute and fluffy rather than something filled with maddening silences and unfathomable secrets.

Like Dr. Jamison.

And I'm just now realizing—right this very second— that while Bruce can raise my heart rate if he really puts his back into it and occasionally borrows a forklift to help him out as needed, my heart rate will soar into the red zone if someone else so much as mentions Dr. Jamison's name in my presence.

Those are all bad signs, aren't they?

I try to pay attention to the proceedings, feeling increasingly flustered.

"Are you also a doc?" Dr. Jamison asks Bruce as he lets go of his hand.

"Corporate lawyer down in D.C.," Bruce says with an exuberance that emphasizes that the beer in his hand is not his first of the night or even his third, blissfully unaware that he's in the process of being graded on anything. "Up for the weekend."

"Well." Dr. Jamison's attention leaves Bruce and

returns to me. I experience that same undefinable jolt of something that I always feel when our gazes connect, despite the fact that his expression is as implacable as it ever was. The Sphinx remains true to form after all these years. As does my unsupported but persistent feeling that there are things he would tell me if only he could. Things he *wants* to tell me. "I'll get out of your hair. Let you kids enjoy your date night."

He nods and walks off, leaving me alone with Bruce while I wage a private battle with disappointment. If the part of me that wishes she'd never see Dr. Jamison again waged a battle with the part of me that wants to call him back and demand he finish asking me that question, I think they would kill each other in a draw.

But Bruce is watching me. I'm older and wiser now. I'm with an available man who genuinely cares about me. I refuse to let old patterns repeat themselves.

So I force myself to smile, an effort that requires every bit of my strength and control short of reaching up and using my thumb and forefinger to push the corners of my mouth into position.

"Cheers to a beautiful night," I say, raising my glass.

"Cheers to *you*." We clink as he gives me an appreciative once-over that lingers on my mouth before dipping to my swelling cleavage and back up again. My girls have been strapped into my gown via Spanx. I chose something empire-waisted for tonight, a style that's universally flattering even to women like me, who carry an extra, oh, let's call it twenty pounds, but you can only demand so much of your support wear. In another couple of hours, all this cleavage is going to *sproing* free like soda escaping from a shaken two-liter bottle. I go to the gym and have recently started jogging (not well, but consistently), but those efforts haven't yielded fruit just yet. "You look amazing."

See? That's one of the best things about Bruce. He thinks I'm beautiful and he expresses it. Constantly. He doesn't seem to see my extra weight at all. Not that I am my dress size, but you know what I mean. He's not like other men I've dated, or tried to date, one of whom actually said, and this is a direct quote from when I walked into the bar and introduced myself, "I don't want to waste your time. Plus-sized isn't my thing."

Bruce is a great guy. Not a jerk temporarily disguised as a great guy so he can get laid. A truly great guy.

Yet here I am, badly rattled by the reappearance of the married, standoffish and infuriating Dr. Jamison. A man I thought I was over by now. A man I *should* be over by now.

Honestly, I feel like I should tell Bruce he could do so much better than me. Actually, strike that. I feel like I should do so much better for Bruce. He deserves it.

"No, *you* look amazing," I say.

His smile slips away, leaving something unexpectedly serious.

"*What?*" I ask, bemused.

"Have I mentioned how glad I am to have you in my life?"

"Aww. Me too," I say.

It's true. Thanks to Bruce, I'm off the dating hamster wheel and no longer need to spend chunks of my time running and spinning only to get the same sorry results. Now that Bruce and I are together, I have a companion. A team. Someone who has my back along with my Friday nights, Saturday mornings and holidays. A nice and funny guy with his own career who understands my endless hours at the hospital. For the first time in my life, I'm with the kind of person who might make someone a great daddy one day. I have that mythical marvel, as rare as a sighting of Zeus on top of One World Trade Center —a good man who's willing and able to commit.

I'm not so lonely now. Thanks to Bruce. He's living, breathing proof that I don't always suck at selecting objects of my affection. And that I am a little bit special. Special enough to catch the interest of a great guy, anyway. Yeah, yeah, I know I'm special on paper. My self-esteem may have training wheels on it, but it manages to stay upright most of the time. I know that I'm smart. Accomplished. Funny. Pretty.

But has a decent guy ever thought that I was *special*? Before Bruce clicked on my profile pic and reached out to me?

I don't think so.

He drinks more than I do, but that's okay, right? No one is perfect. I eat more dessert than he does. So what? And if things with Bruce are a tiny bit predictable and a tinier bit boring every now and then, isn't that a small price to pay? Isn't that how it goes when you're building a solid relationship?

Yeah. I think it is.

"I was hoping you'd say that," he says, grinning.

"If I can just pass my boards and land a fellowship, my life will be pretty much perfect," I add.

"Funny you should mention that." He hesitates, clearing his throat as two bright patches of color concentrate in his cheeks and his smile fades away. "I've been thinking."

Something in his new expression gives me a funny feeling. "Do tell."

"A position opened up in the firm's Manhattan office. I thought I'd apply for it."

I freeze, the bottom falling out of my thoughts.

"D.C. and New York have reciprocity, so I wouldn't have to take the bar exam again," he continues quickly. "I don't know about you, but I've had enough of the long-distance thing. What do you think?"

I somehow get my mouth to open but take several long beats to get it working beyond that.

"Oh my God," I finally say. "I had no idea you were thinking about anything like that."

"Now you know."

"But…" I smooth my hair away from my face with my free hand, trying hard to diagnose my feelings about this surprise. Joy? Relief? Alarm? Some cocktail of all three? Whatever they are, they don't match the look of bright happiness on his face. "It's so soon. We've only been together for six months. That's not very long."

"How long is long enough?"

Longer than this, I want to say.

"I don't know," I say instead. "I have much more experience with men who don't want to commit to anything more than a couple of nights a week."

"We've been doing a couple of nights a week. I think we can do better."

I squint my mind's eye, trying to imagine him and the contents of his apartment squeezing into my one-bedroom Murray Hill apartment. Let's just say that it's not a fit.

"So…Are you talking about us, what, getting an apartment together?" I ask.

"Well, yeah. The idea is for us to spend more time together."

"Yeah, but I'll still be working all the time whether you're here or still in D.C.," I remind him. I don't know why I feel this strange compulsion to talk him out of the exact thing that most dating women of childbearing age want. "That won't change."

"I get that. But I'll still see you a hell of a lot more than eight days out of the month."

"But…you love D.C."

"I love New York, too," he says, shrugging easily, then downs the rest of his beer.

"What about your lease?"

"It's up in a couple of months."

"Oh," I say faintly.

He takes a closer look at me. The kind of look for which I am definitely ill-prepared at the moment. All that bright happiness evaporates.

"It was just an idea," he says dully. "Forget I said anything. We don't have to if you're not ready."

Is *that* what this sensation is? That I'm not ready? I try the feeling on for size but can't decide whether it's a fit or not. I open my mouth, but another delay kicks in, one that makes my ambivalence all the more awkward.

"Whoa," he says, eyes widening. "You don't see yourself going any further with me? Is that it?"

"No," I say, the suggestion jarring me into action. I want to get married one day when the time is right. Bruce checks all the appropriate boxes. Of course I've thought about taking next steps with him. But the next steps were always at some vague and indeterminate point in the future, when things in my life were…I don't know. More settled, I guess. Like when I knew where I'd have my fellowship, for instance. "That's not it at all. I'm just surprised. You've been thinking about this already. I just

need time to get my mind around it and figure out the logistics. That's all."

His expression clears. "That's all? You sure?"

I blink and crank my reassuring smile into place. "Absolutely."

"So you're open to the idea? And to me pursuing the transfer?"

"Of course I am."

"Good," he says, coming in for a kiss before sliding his lips around to my ear. "Because I'm starting to have serious feelings for you."

The ear thing gets me every time, I admit. I soften, wondering what the hell is wrong with me tonight. Bruce and I are taking next steps, which is what grownups do. Hallelujah for that.

"Good," I say, grinning as I let him reel me in.

3

MICHAEL

"WHAT'S THE PROBLEM?"

I'm over at the bar, nursing a foul mood and waiting for my second scotch and soda, when Jake finds me a few minutes later. Having just witnessed Ally and her *boyfriend* engage in their display of public affection — I'm a glutton for punishment; what can I say? — all I want to do is wallow in bitterness and self-pity until this godforsaken boat returns to shore and I can slink home in peace. I'm not much of a drinker, but tonight seems like the ideal time to rectify that.

In short? Now is not the time for Jake and his stupid questions.

"There's no problem," I tell Jake.

"Are we going to grab a plate or not? They opened the buffet, but you're out here navel-gazing."

"You go ahead. I'll grab something in a minute."

Jake frowns at me. "Since when do *you* miss meals?"

"It's not a big deal," I say with a grateful nod at the bartender as he hands me my refill and I drop a tip into his jar. "I'll catch up."

"I get it," Jake says, nodding sagely. "Your little reunion didn't go as planned?"

I think about my soaring but irrational hopes for this evening. My equally illogical disappointment as said hopes got incinerated in a white-hot flash of bad timing and thwarted desire. I think about how some other guy belongs in Ally's bed, and I still do not and probably never will. I briefly consider the possibility of solving the problem by flipping the guy over the railing when the chance presents itself, then remind myself that a) at least a hundred people would witness the assault because I'm not the smooth criminal type; and b) indulging my seething jealousy is probably not worth the potential risks to my career and freedom.

Which leaves me with drinking and brooding as my only other alternatives.

"It did not," I say, my voice clipped.

"That's a shame," Jake says, following my line of sight to the table about fifty feet away where Ally and the guy are eating. "She's easy on the eyes."

"That she is."

Let's go ahead and classify that as the understatement of the century.

That bombshell body. That hair. Those *eyes*.

I know I don't get a woman just because she's beautiful and I want her. Or even because I *really* want her. That's not how the world works. Ally gets a say in the matter, not that I've ever even told her how I feel. Hell, maybe she hates my guts. And on top of that, she has a boyfriend. Understood.

But *fuck*.

I've fantasized about her for so long. Thought about her so many times over the years.

I didn't get divorced because of her. And I'm not looking to get into a whole big thing with someone new right now, even her. But I'm *free* now. And I really hoped I'd have the opportunity to spend a little time with her. To explore the connection I thought we'd felt back then. Just to satisfy my curiosity, if nothing else.

Now it's not going to happen.

Is this the end of the world? No. Will I survive? Yes.

Do I *want* to survive at this dark moment? Questionable.

Stifling a curse, I down my new drink in a couple of rough gulps, then put the empty glass back on the bar and signal for the bartender once again.

Thanks for the kick in the teeth, God.

Thanks. For. Nothing.

Jake watches me with poorly concealed amusement. "How's ruining your liver going to solve anything?" he says.

"What else am I going to do until the boat docks?"

"There are plenty of other beautiful women on the boat," he says, incredulous. "Don't tell me you hadn't noticed."

I shrug, saying nothing.

If he doesn't want me to tell him, then I won't. But I hadn't noticed.

"Why don't you flash your wallet at one of them? Enjoy yourself and stop acting like a loser."

The mere suggestion leaves a bad taste in my mouth.

"Let's just say the bloom's off that rose," I say.

As a newly divorced guy, I've enjoyed my share of hooking up lately, I admit it. But you can only swipe right so many times and make idle chitchat with complete strangers at bars as a prelude to having one-off sex before it hits you: it's not that great. Oh, sure, the theoretical idea that you could have sex with any willing woman who catches your eye is great. In practice? Not so much. How much lame conversation are you willing to endure before either calling it a night or suggesting an adjournment to someone's apartment or a hotel room? Fifteen minutes? Half an hour? What do you say after you've done the deed? How long should you stick around? Should you act like you're interested in more when you usually aren't?

I have alternatives. I get that. All the women in the world aren't tied to some dating app. Women make eyes at me at the gym and the hospital all the time. But why piss in your own swimming pool? I don't want to get glared at every time I go to the cafeteria at work just because I didn't call someone the next day.

I don't have the time or energy to deal with all this crap every time I want to get laid. It's exhausting. And my career is already exhausting enough, thanks.

The whole dating thing, man. Fraught with peril.

"So what does the guy do?" Jake asks thoughtfully, still staring at the couple.

"Lawyer."

"I hate him already," he says with a scowl, which is the only acceptable response a doctor can give when confronted with a lawyer.

"Indeed," I say, nodding my thanks at the bartender for my latest refill.

"Have they been married long?" Jake asks.

"Oh, they're not married." I take a measured sip this time, deciding to pace myself. "He lives down in —"

"Wait, wait, wait, wait, *wait*. *What?*" Jake gapes at me

as though I've suggested a date with yonder Lady Liberty. "They're not married?"

"No," I say, startled by all the sudden vehemence.

"Then why the fuck are you over here acting like you're about to jump overboard?"

"Because they're in a committed relationship," I say, wondering why that needs to be said and what I'm missing.

"A committed—?" He can barely get the words out. "Are you *insane*?"

"No," I say, my ears starting to burn, although I'm not sure whether it's from anger or embarrassment. "A commitment's a commitment."

Jake stares at me for a second or two then bursts into a round of raucous laughter that culminates with him doubling over and bracing his hands on his thighs for support.

I, meanwhile, stand there seething impotently—yeah, it's definitely *anger*—and decide that if I get the opportunity to push anyone overboard tonight, it's going to be Jake rather than Ally's boyfriend.

"Will you stop being such a choirboy? For once?" he says as he collects himself enough to straighten and wipe his streaming eyes. "Jesus Christ, wait till I tell Liam about this."

Ladies and gentlemen, introducing my other nickname. Choirboy.

"I don't get the joke," I snap. Commitments mean something, as I know from painful personal experience. I was tempted back when I was married, but I didn't cheat. I did the right thing and stood by my vows as a husband. Which mature adults are supposed to do when they possess a working moral compass. "Fill me in."

"You're standing here like she's this forbidden fruit, Mikey. But she's not even married. *You* were married. *That's* forbidden. But you're talking about a *boyfriend*? Hell, she's not even engaged. For all you know, she just started dating this clown two weeks ago. And you want to sacrifice your big chance for *that*? Don't be a dope, choirboy. The way I see it? The way most men see it? She's fair game. Fair. Game."

I frown while this novel idea reverberates through my moralistic brain.

Do the right thing, Mikey is the soundtrack by which my upstanding parents raised me and my sister, their precious children, of whom much was given and much was expected. *Don't screw it up.*

No lying. No cheating. Be kind. Work hard. Keep your word.

That pretty much covers every lesson they ever taught us.

And yet...

"Yeah, but—" I begin.

"Yeah, but nothing," he says. "Don't try to tell me you owe that guy anything. You don't know him. And if he hasn't put a ring on it yet, that's on him."

I feel a wild swoop of hopeful excitement but do my best to rein it in.

"Yeah, but I'm not trying to blow anyone's shit up," I say. "That's bad karma."

"Relax. If their relationship is as rock solid as it needs to be, nothing you do will hurt it."

That's what I'm afraid of.

"That sounds like the kind of thing people tell themselves to justify bad behavior," I say darkly. "Like the bank robber who says, 'Yeah, but they shouldn't have left the vault unlocked.'"

"Yeah, okay. You know what's bad karma? Letting a golden opportunity pass you by and then *still* having this woman on your mind in *another* four years. Think about *that*."

The idea generates an involuntary grimace. Four more years of thinking about Ally? Of wondering what she's doing and whether she ever thought about me the way I thought about her?

Trust me when I tell you that I'm not built for that.

"That's what I thought," he says with grim satisfaction, successfully reading my expression once again. An annoying habit that both he and Liam possess in spades. "You have my permission to go for it. Now I'm done with this conversation. I'm not going to let your ridiculous ethics cause me to starve when they're serving prime rib and shrimp in there. Peace."

With that, he strides off, leaving me to marinate in my own juices while I process his advice and try to figure out next steps. Part of my problem is that my body has a violently negative reaction to the possibility that Jake could be right about anything. Ever. Sure, he's a brilliant doctor these days, as well as being one of my business partners and longstanding best friends. But I still remember the unholy mess he made back when we were freshman at NYU. He downed one too many lime Jell-O shots and yakked it back up through his nose. My philosophy since then has been that anyone who listens to *that* guy's advice does so at his or her own peril.

But…could he be right? This one time?

The questions distract me all through dinner and the remainder of the cruise.

Even more distracting? The sight of Ally. Her presence again after all this time. Just knowing that she's here. Close enough for me to feel the crackle of her electricity through the air, as though she's a storm approaching on the other side of my horizon. The thunder and lightning haven't fully geared up yet, but they're coming. It's only a matter of time.

I say my goodbyes to Jake and wander down the gangplank and over to the end of the valet line at the end of the night, thinking that she's always had this effect on me.

From the very first time I met her.

4

MICHAEL

"HARLOW?" I glance up from my notes and wait for a response, but none comes. All I see are a bunch of eager but otherwise vapid faces that look as though they belong to twelve-year-olds who've all decided to dress up as doctors for Halloween. "Where the hell is Harlow?"

Running footsteps approach behind me.

"Here," comes a breathless female voice. "I'm here."

I turn, frowning.

To be fair, my mood was already shot before this first-year resident, a.k.a. intern, showed up two minutes late for work. Sure, it's great to be chief resident, but the problem with the position is the younger residents, who are uniformly stupid, annoying and likely to kill any vulnerable patients who have the misfortune of crossing their paths. Plus, I had a fight with my wife last night because I fell asleep during our date-night Broadway musical and evidently snored through most of the last fifteen minutes of Hamilton. So I'm just looking for someone to kill, and that may as well be this idiot resident who's not even smart enough to show up to work on time. No one will miss her anyway.

"Rounds start at five thirty, Harlow," I say, turning so I can

hit her with the full force of my ferocity. "Not five thirty-two. See
the difference?"

"Sorry." *The voice is bright and utterly devoid of remorse.*
"Sometimes I get sick before big events. First day of medical
school. Taking my boards. First day of residency. I'm good now,
though. I just needed to find some mouthwash."

The other interns titter.

*I gape at her, trapped inside my multilayered stupefaction.
First, because she's so completely unbothered. The cutthroat world
of surgeons in the making is inhabited by sharks, piranhas,
pirates and anyone or anything else that would kill you as soon
as look at you. People around here do not help each other out or
admit to weaknesses. They do not laugh unless they're making
fun of their colleagues and competitors. On pain of death.*

*Second, because something about the situation (me?) seems
to amuse her.*

*Third, because now that I get a good look at her, I see that
she's fucking gorgeous.*

*She's got a fresh-faced, sparkly-eyed girl-next-door aura
going on, the kind that guarantees laughter and mischief. The
kind that makes you want to stick around so you won't miss
anything. On top of that, she's rocking a bombshell body under
her white lab coat and sunshiny yellow scrubs. I can tell. Surgical
scrubs aren't exactly bikinis in terms of highlighting the female
form, but men are men, and we notice women. If you're a married
man like me, you do it discreetly and never follow up on it, but
you still notice. I've already noticed the blond resident's long legs,
for example. The redhead's ass.*

Noted and dismissed.

But this one.

She's got the boobs. The ass. The hair. The eyes.

The radiance.

This one makes the hair on my nape prickle and shows

every sign of being able to get under my skin. Which is not what I'm about, in my personal life or my professional life. I'll have to work a bit harder than usual to squash my budding attraction to her. Luckily, I'm a master of both compartmentalizing my feelings and icy disdain. Time to put both skills to work.

"Harlow."

"Sir?"

"No one gives a fuck about your gastric habits. Barf earlier. Be on time."

"Will do," she says with an unmistakable gleam of amusement.

"Something funny?" I bark, watching her with unwilling fascination.

"Not at all."

"You don't seem to care that you're putting a target on your own damn back right out of the gate," I say, generating around of sniggering among the other residents.

The smile slips away from her laughing eyes for the first time. "My best friend Kelly suffered from third-degree burns from a kitchen accident when we were kids. She *had* a target on her back. *This*, I can deal with."

Whoa.

Another vulnerability revealed by young Dr. Harlow.

Another corresponding prickle of awareness across my scalp.

Another tug of longing inside me.

More importantly, another opportunity for me to reinforce my shields.

"Fascinating," I say in my most scathing tone. "Any other true confessions? Or can we get to patient care now that you've wasted five minutes of our time?"

"You're in charge," she says without missing a beat.

But she's wrong.

I've never been in charge of a single interaction I've had with her.

If I were in charge of anything, I wouldn't have approached her in the hospital café at lunch that day, when I saw her studying the Greek yogurt selections with more concentration than I've seen some of my colleagues use during brain surgery.

"Just pick one, Harlow," I say, sliding into place behind her in the world's longest line and selecting a cup of strawberry. "You're not defusing a bomb here."

"Dr. Jamison," she says, startled. "It's not that easy. I'm trying to figure out my point situation."

"Point situation?"

"I'm celebrating my fifth anniversary of trying to lose the same twenty pounds," she says with a grimace, finally grabbing a cup of vanilla. "This yogurt selection is going to make all the difference."

I can't help but smile, which troubles me greatly. First, because I hate being pleasant to interns. Second, because I find her openness refreshing. Third, and this is the biggie, because the idea of her trying to tweak this *body is the most ridiculous thing I've ever heard. Where would she take the pounds from? Her stellar ass? Her generous boobs? Why would she do that? What if Rubens had painted over all his voluptuous nudes and thinned them down? Is that the kind of thing the world should be grateful for? I don't think so.*

"That's stupid," I say.

"What?" she says, frowning up at me. "Being healthy?"

"Obsessing over nonsense," I say, selecting a banana as the line sidles forward.

"Well, thank you for that unsolicited opinion about my obsession, Dr. Jamison," she says with a repressive sidelong glare. "Isn't there a rule against the chief being abusive to interns on our lunch break?"

I can't help but chuckle.

"Absolutely not. You're lucky I don't send you to track down some labs for me. Ruin your lunch altogether just for fun."

"Wonderful. Don't let me keep you from harassing my colleagues. They're at the table over there," she says, gesturing.

"In a minute." I grab some bottled water and choose my words with care. "What happened to her? Your friend."

She'd been selecting a fruit cup, but now she glances up at me, looking surprised.

I feel the connection in the pit of my belly. There's something extraordinary about these brown eyes.

"Kelly. She had third-degree burns on her face and neck. She had surgeries. Grafts. More surgeries. She's doing well now, but she really suffered."

I nod with complete understanding because I've treated dozens of Kellys in my career. "Ah."

"That's why I want to be a plastic surgeon," she continues. "To help kids like her. But also because we've got to do better for kids like her."

"Better?" I say, arrested by this new fervency.

"Better skin grafts. Better reconstruction. Better pain management. All of it."

Here's another annoying thing about interns: their relentless idealism and optimism. It's the solemn duty of older doctors like me to beat it out of them. Modern medicine can do a lot, but it can't do everything. We can't save every patient or even improve the life of every patient. Patients suffer. Some die. And the contributions of us doctors, even the great ones, of which there are far too few, won't change that reality.

But there's something about hearing this kind of thing from Harlow that touches me as much as it amuses me.

"Pace yourself. This is your first day. You won't know what kind of surgeon you want to be until you've tried a few."

Her jaw tightens as she stares me in the face.

"Here's the thing about me, Dr. Jamison. I know what I want."

I come out of my daydream to realize that the valet line has barely shuffled forward a couple of feet.

I know what I want, she said.

Wish *I* did.

To do the right thing or not. That is the question.

I sigh, roll my shoulders, try to work a couple of kinks out of my neck—

And spot her standing about thirty feet away, fiddling with her purse and evidently waiting for good old Bruce to bring the car around for her. Her face is downturned. Pensive.

I stare, a spider caught in my own web of longing and ambivalence. I would give a million dollars of my new fortune to know what she's thinking right now. I would give two million if someone could verify that I figure anywhere in her thoughts.

Abandoning my spot in line and thereby dooming myself to not getting home for another hour or more, I head over to her. I keep my hands in my pockets because I don't know what else to do with them, and I can't swear that they wouldn't reach for her if given half the chance.

She hears my approach and glances up, looking wary.

"Enjoy the cruise?" I ask.

"I did," she says. "They ran out of the cocktail shrimp by the time I got through the line, but you can't have everything."

Can't have everything. Ain't that the truth?

"He seems nice," I force myself to say. "Bruce."

"He is," she says, smiling.

I try to figure out whether it's a standard small-talk smile or a wildly-in-love smile and can't quite decide.

"Been together long?" I ask.

"About six months."

"Ah." I work several frantic calculations in my brain, trying to figure out what that means in terms of relationship seriousness. Living together? Exchanged *I love yous*? Met each other's families? Discussed the future? Who the hell knows? "Did I hear him say he's from D.C.?"

"You did. Although he may be moving to the city. We'll see."

We'll. See.

Why does it feel like those two flimsy words carry the weight of my entire existence?

I try to generate something congratulatory to say and get as far as opening my mouth before she interrupts me.

"Listen," she says, turning to face me as her tone acquires a new urgency. "You're back now, and we may be seeing each other here and there at the hospital. I don't want things to be awkward. I just want to apologize for what I, ah, said the last time I saw you. And the way I, ah, threw myself at you."

I freeze, my thoughts catapulting back to that night at the bar. To what she said. The way she looked and her passion when she said it. To my own spiraling feelings and the way I ruthlessly repressed them the way modern medicine ruthlessly repressed smallpox and polio.

"You want to apologize?" I ask, my throat tightening. This parking-lot conversation has taken an interesting and unexpected turn. Yes, indeed.

"It was a rough day for me," she continues, a flush climbing over her cheeks. "I'd been drinking margaritas and I'm not normally a big drinker. The point is, it wasn't my best moment. I don't know. Maybe you've forgotten all about it by now."

Not a chance in hell.

"Maybe I shouldn't even bring it up at this late date. But I don't want you to think badly of me. So…" She takes a deep breath. "I'm sorry I was disrespectful to your marriage. It'll never happen again. And it would've never happened in the first place if I hadn't been drinking so much that night."

Well, now, hang on.

I cock my head and squint at her, determined to make sure I'm getting these important details right.

"So…you didn't mean it?"

She forces a smile and her expression locks into place. I see it happen as though she's posing for a picture and waiting for the photographer to click the shutter.

"Of course not."

I stiffen.

The voice in my head, meanwhile, grabs a megaphone and shouts in my ear.

Bullshit.

I don't believe her. Not for a second. I heard what she said that night in the bar. Much as I tried to hide it at the time, it meant something to me. Still means something to me, as a matter of fact. She can't yank the rug out from under me by taking it all back now. Not when we've got unfinished business that I'm dying to resume.

I open my mouth to call her on it but stop myself. Now is not the time. And this is not the place. Not with her boyfriend due to make an appearance any second.

But it's all good. Our time will come. Soon.

Little does she know that she's just goaded me out of

my ambivalence and helped me formulate a plan. With apologies to Bruce, who seems like a nice enough guy. But fuck him. I don't owe him anything. I owe it to Ally and myself to get to the bottom of this vibe between us once and for all.

I know just how I'm going to do it. And I *don't* plan to screw it up.

"So you *didn't* mean what you said," I say pleasantly. "Good to know. That clears *everything* up."

"Really?" she says, brightening.

I hesitate.

If only she knew how badly I want her thighs wrapped around my waist and her tongue in my mouth. Right this very second.

"A hundred percent."

"Good," she says with a relieved smile. "So…how *is* your wife?"

"No idea," I say, maintaining eye contact for the sheer pleasure of watching that smile shrivel up and die as I hit her with my news. "We got divorced last year."

5

ALLY

MY PHONE BUZZES RIGHT AROUND three the following Wednesday afternoon, just as I'm hurrying across the skywalk from the hospital to the medical arts building. I pull it out and check the display without breaking stride, relieved to discover that it's my best friend Kelly, with whom I've been playing phone tag for the last couple of days. I never know how to feel about breaking events in my life until running things by her, and God knows I need her input now.

It's been an eventful forty-eight hours. To say the least.

"Hey," she says when the picture resolves to reveal her sitting behind the wheel of her parked car. She eyeballs my scrubs. "In between surgeries?"

"On my way to a meeting, actually."

"I'll talk fast, then. What's this I hear about Bruce moving to the Big Apple?"

"He says he wants to take things to the next level," I say, grinning. Even though I've had time to get used to the idea by now, I still can't quite keep the amazement out of my voice. I think it's because a part of me never believed that I could actually do it—find a guy who likes me enough and thinks I'm special enough to get serious. With all the snakes and losers I've dated over the years? All the men who are intimidated by my MD? All the men who think that my MD is cool and all but still expect me to happily suspend my career advancement in favor of *theirs*? All the men who prefer toned and athletic size sixes? Please. I feel like a baby bird that's finally hopped out of the nest and discovered that she could fly.

"I told you he was a good guy." Kelly beams at me with the exact level of enthusiasm you'd expect from a great best friend. "Are you excited?"

I want to say of course I am, but something invisible holds me back.

"Hang on," she says, her smile fading. "What's with the face?"

"I think I'm a little shell-shocked," I confess. "We haven't been dating all that long. It's a big step."

"Yeah, but when you know you know, right? Why waste time? Especially at our age."

Well, that's certainly true. I'm pushing thirty-two. While I'm not exactly knocking on death's door, I've learned enough about maternal fertility issues to know that the landscape for getting pregnant changes after thirty-five. That means I may want to start getting my ducks in a row if I hope to have a couple of kids before it's too late. Which I do.

"You're right," I tell her. "But I'm not picking out china patterns and running to the pharmacy for pregnancy tests just yet. Bruce and I are having initial discussions about the possibility of him moving to New York. It may or may not pan out. He needs to get the job first."

"I've got my fingers and bra straps crossed for you," she says happily. "Just don't go picking out any brides-maids dresses with ruffles or lace or I will kill you. *Kill. You.* Nonnegotiable."

"Your request is noted," I say, laughing as I arrive at the waiting area just outside a huge and swanky suite of offices and have a seat. I check out the elegant lettering over the glass double doors:

Jamison & Associates.

Dr. Jamison's new plastic surgery private practice.

My heart rate kicks up a notch or two.

Or a thousand.

"So what else is going on?" she says.

"Funny you should ask," I say, dropping my voice even though there's no one nearby. "Dr. Jamison is back in town. I saw him Saturday night."

She gives me a blank look. "Who?"

"The Sphinx," I hiss.

"Oh my God," she cries, clapping a hand over her mouth. The poor thing probably hoped to never hear the S-word from my lips again. Having suffered through my obsession with a married man in real time back then, she's probably hit her lifetime limit of talking me down from ledges where he's concerned. Still, she plays along like the good friend that she is. "How does he look?"

"Amazing," I say glumly, mollified that she seems to understand the gravity of the situation. When I mention the Sphinx, I fully expect the same sort of scandalized dismay with which Samantha, Miranda and Charlotte reacted every time Carrie spoke Mr. Big's name in *Sex and the City.* "He's got the tall, dark and handsome thing nailed, only he's handsomer now. He's got, I don't know, these sexy crow's-feet now. And a little gray through the temples. Your basic nightmare."

"Damn," she says sadly. "Seems like he'd gain twenty pounds or go bald or something."

"I know, right?"

"So? I'm guessing you made idle chitchat? How did you feel? Please tell me you're over him."

Meeting her gaze suddenly becomes impossible. "Of course I'm over him," I say irritably, crossing my legs and adjusting my lab coat over my scrubs. "What kind of fool do you take me for?"

Kelly, being smarter than the average bear, clearly doesn't believe me for a second. "Ally…" she says, infusing her voice with just the right note of warning. "Don't do it, girl."

"Of course I'm not going to do it," I say vehemently. "My life is going great right now. I'm in a real relationship with a good guy. For once. Just about to finish up my residency and get my career going. As soon as I pass my boards and line up my fellowship, I'll be good as gold. I'm not going to do anything to screw it up. Including making eyes at the Sphinx. Especially that."

"Good," she says firmly. "Because the last thing you need is another downward spiral over a married man."

Downward spiral.

What a charming euphemism for the depression I battled four years ago, when I let my growing obsession with him get the best of me and needed to take that brief leave of absence to get my head on straight with some counseling and medication. Thank God he moved out west around the same time. Otherwise? I really don't know how I would have gotten over him.

"I'm aware. But he's, ah, divorced now. Just FYI."

"Oh, *shit.*" She leans forward with the intensity of an attending walking me through a dicey portion of an abdominal surgery. "Ally, I don't care whether he's divorced or not. You stay away from him. You've got Bruce now. That's a *real relationship* with potential. The Sphinx is bad for you. He plays head games."

"He never did anything wrong," I say, wondering why I feel this strange compulsion to defend him. "It's not his fault I threw myself at him."

"He sent you mixed messages, Ally."

"He didn't, though," I say, my morale plummeting another couple of notches at this reminder that I never even tempted him despite his profound effect on *me*. Not that I think I'm some modern version of Scheherazade, but still. "He was always a perfect gentleman."

And yet...

There were moments when I felt...

What, Ally?

You can't explain it, can you? Even to yourself. Even now.

There were moments when I felt...that he was watching me. That he was standing closer than he needed to. Staring too long. That he was far too aware of me and what I was doing at any given time. That the air buzzed when we were in a room together. Any room.

That we had a *connection*.

But that's the thing about sexy married men in positions of power, isn't it? Every woman in his orbit probably winds up feeling the same way.

Hell, I don't know. Maybe Kelly's right about the head games. If so, I'm uniquely susceptible to them.

Besides. A man like *that*—smart, sexy, billionaire— isn't thinking about a woman like *me*—cute, a little too curvy, occasionally bitchy—when he could have *anyone*.

And the sooner I get that through my thick skull and get Dr. Jamison out of my head, the happier I'll be.

"I'm planning to stay far away from him," I tell her, meaning it.

"Good," she says, not bothering to hide her relief. "It's a big hospital, right? And you'll be going somewhere else soon for your fellowship. You won't have to see him at all, I'm hoping."

"I won't have to see him at all," I say, bracing myself for her reaction. "After this meeting I'm about to go into."

Unmitigated horror from Kelly. "Wait, *what*? What meeting? What does he want?"

"No idea. He texted me a little while ago."

"Well, what does it say?"

I scroll over to the message so I can give her a direct quote: "It says, 'Stop by my office after three. Thanks.'"

"Ally, you can't just come running every time that arrogant SOB snaps his fingers," she says with a bit more exasperation than I think is strictly necessary.

Easy for her to say. She doesn't understand that, as interns, we were trained to come running every time our chief resident so much as thought our names. We were all like Pavlov's dogs by the end of the year. Besides which, the female side of me is dying of curiosity to see what he could possibly want.

"Agreed. This is a one-off," I say, standing. "Gotta go."

"Keep me posted."

"Will do," I say, then I hang up and head into the suite.

The empty reception area has that fresh paint smell. It still has moving boxes stacked around the perimeter but manages to look as though it belongs to some chic boutique hotel, with boxy modern chairs and striking minimalist artwork on the walls. The windows provide a great view of Bryant Park. I can only imagine that the ladies-who-lunch set from the Upper East Side will stream here in droves, like pilgrims to a shine. This is all money in the bank for Dr. Jamison, who may as well have set up a printing press for thousand-dollar bills in one of his back rooms.

"Hi," I say, approaching the receptionist at her window, where she's arranging items on her desk. "I'm Ally Harlow here to see —"

A door a few feet away swings open without warning. Dr. Jamison appears, looking as handsome and imperious as ever in his lab coat and scrubs and generating a corresponding adrenaline surge inside me.

"Harlow," he calls. "You're late. Tick-tock."

I check my watch. One past three.

I thank the receptionist and head his way, not bothering to hide my scowl as I ease past him into the inner area, which features exam rooms and offices around a central nurses' station. The place is a hive of activity, with people scurrying to unpack and organize supplies.

It's elegant. Cutting edge. The ideal office setup, if you ask me.

But I need to stay focused. I need to say my piece, find out what he wants and get the hell out of here before I relapse into obsession. I've got to avoid him at all costs. That's the key.

I take a deep breath and hike up my chin, determined to stand my ground and remember that I'm no longer a peon. I'm also determined to ignore the subtly woodsy scent of his skin—he's way too close—and its effect on my impressionable lady parts.

"Okay, first of all, you invited me to stop by *after* three," I say. "Which I am doing. Second, I'm no longer on your service. I'm actually a fully grown medical professional now. Maybe you should remember that the next time you command me to show up at your office."

"Old habits die hard," he says, demonstrating zero signs of actual remorse. "How do you like my setup?"

"It's amazing. You must be so excited." Arrogant as he is, I don't bother trying to hide my delight at his accomplishments. He's worked hard and earned everything he has. I can't take that away from him. "Congratulations. I'm thrilled for you. And congratulations on selling your medical device. You've been busy the last few years, haven't you?"

He doesn't quite smile, but a gleam of quiet pride commandeers his face.

I stare, arrested.

Swear to God, there's no legal reason why anyone should be this sexy and handsome. It's just not normal. It's like beholding twinkling starlight in a bottle. There's just no getting used to it no matter how much you try.

"Thanks," he says gruffly. "Wasn't sure you'd heard about that."

I hesitate because I can't decide whether there's a veiled question in there or not. If there is, I'd rather not admit that of course I've followed his career and press coverage. To tell the truth, if I spent as much time on my exercise bike as I did scrolling through articles about him and his medical innovations, I wouldn't still be worried about those twenty stubborn pounds.

"That kind of news travels fast," I say, my cheeks and ears burning.

"Ah."

"So when do you start seeing patients?" I ask as he leads me down the hallway.

"Monday."

"*Monday*. Are you excited?"

He cocks his head and squints as he thinks it over. "I am. I'm looking forward to doing some good in the world."

"Good. You've been such a slacker up until now," I say gravely.

"Private bathroom with shower and sauna for the docs," he says, grinning as he points.

"Nice."

He keeps going and turns the corner into an office.

"Oh, it's *beautiful*," I cry, taking a good look around as he sits behind the desk and I sit in front of it. Another great view of Bryant Park and the public library. Walls painted a pale but cheerful yellow that's the exact color of my favorite pair of scrubs back when I was an intern. And the artwork? A giant framed print of one of Monet's water lily paintings. "I *love* Monet. I used to have a waterlily scrub cap."

His brows go up. "Really?"

"Really," I say. "But back to you. I hope you're not going to spend every day on facelifts and breast augmentations."

"Why not?" he says, his interest sharpening. "Don't you believe in paying the bills? And beautifying the world by straightening noses and lifting eyelids?"

"You have plenty of money to pay your bills now," I say tartly. "And the resources to—"

"What? Help kids who've been burned like your friend Kelly? Work on better reconstruction procedures? Better skin grafts and pain management?"

"Exactly," I say, startled by his memory of something I mentioned once years ago. Although I shouldn't be. Having worked closely with him, I know exactly how brilliant he is. I wouldn't be surprised if he has a photographic memory. "I think that's more important than eradicating neck wattles on the Upper East Side."

"Agreed. And that's what my team and I plan to do. State-of-the-art stuff."

I can't stop a grin from exploding across my face. If a man with Dr. Jamison's skills and resources puts his mind to it, he'll make great strides in the area. I know it. "Really?"

"Really."

"Good," I say, lapsing into a wistful daydream about how great it would be to work at a place exactly like *this*. A place with the vision, the resources and the intrepid leader to bring it all together. Oh, man. What I wouldn't give.

"Glad you approve," he says. "When can you start?"

I blink and refocus on him, slow to come out of my spiraling fantasies. "Start what?"

"Your fellowship."

My breath stops. I mean stops *dead*, as though someone pulled the plug on the ventilator supplying me with air. I manage to crank my mouth open, but that's as far as I get at first.

"I don't have a fellowship," I say carefully.

"Try to keep up, Harlow," he says, giving me a pointed look. "What do you think just happened here?"

I frown and glance around, desperately asking myself

the same question. "I think you just showed me around your office," I say, my voice pitching higher.

"Sorry," he says, managing to look zero percent sorry and one hundred percent smug. "Thought I mentioned this was a job interview. That explains the scrubs. *I* would've worn a suit, but whatever."

This was a — ?

"You know very well that you didn't tell me this was a *job interview*," I say.

"My mistake."

Oh. My. God.

I press my hands to the top of my head in a futile attempt to slow down my racing thoughts and grab one to hold on to. I'm not this lucky. Opportunities of a life-time don't just fall into my lap.

So that's one thing.

The other thing?

The idea of working with him again thrills me as much as it terrifies me. Heavy-handed arrogance and occasional bullying aside (and those traits describe *every* surgeon, frankly), he's a great teacher. I'd learn so much. I'm positive of that. As for keeping my latent feelings for him under control? Questionable. I might even go so far as to give that a poor prognosis.

And that's the bottom line here: I can't work for him. For my own good.

Not that I can tell *him* that.

"It wouldn't work," I say, trying to keep at least *some* of the regret out of my voice. "I'm not in the market to work with someone who'd treat me like an indentured servant. Which is how you see me."

"I get that you're no longer my intern. Trust me," he says, watching me with that implacable gaze of his. "But it sounds like you'd need a complete personality transplant from me."

"I'm not working for you, but no. Not *complete*. Just less reign of terror. More collegial."

"How much less?" he asks.

I think that over. Why not? This is all make-believe anyway. "Seventy-five percent."

"I can do fifty."

I laugh. At least he's self-aware. "I would have settled for thirty," I say. "Not that I'm working for you."

A glint of wicked amusement from him. "I would have given you eighty to seal the deal. And this is *your* office, by the way."

My heart contracts. Hard.

I glance around again, loving the yellow and the Monet. The *view*.

"*My* office?"

"If you want it," he says, shrugging.

If I—

This time I can't even get my mouth open. I have no words. No hope of words.

There's no room for words to coexist with the sudden soaring hope inside me.

I think of the special misery of trying to land a fellowship in plastic surgery, which has the distinction of being one of the most competitive fields in medicine. I think of all the interviews and the weeks and months of uncertainty about which city and hospital I might land in. I think that this setup is beyond my wildest dreams in terms of both fit and opportunity.

Most importantly, I think that this is all too good to be true. Events in my life just don't come together like this, so I'd better not get my hopes up.

I decide to focus on the obvious. "We haven't even discussed salary."

He doesn't say a word. He gives me a narrowed look instead, reaching out and grabbing a sticky note with the dramatic flourish of a conductor walking on stage and raising his baton at the beginning of an orchestra concert. He scrawls several numbers, pauses to frown and consider what he's written, then conspicuously adds another zero before passing the note to me.

I gape at him, heart thundering out of control.

He leans back in his chair, laces his fingers across his taut belly and raises a brow, waiting.

I finally look down at the number. And gasp.

I can't help it.

A number like *this* is life changing. A number like this will help me pay off a huge chunk of my student loan debts in the next year, even while living in one of the most expensive cities in the world. A number like this will allow me to replace my geriatric Camry if I want to and pay cash for something new. A number like this is beyond my most absurd fantasies at this early stage of my career.

I glance up with a thousand questions at the ready, only to hesitate when I see how closely he's watching me. Most of my thoughts scatter, leaving only the one big issue.

Am I a good surgeon and getting better every day? Sure. But I'm not *this* special.

"Why would you pay me this kind of money?" I ask.

He hesitates. His expression becomes so still and inscrutable that I decide that whoever nicknamed him the Sphinx was a fucking genius. My intuition whispers that whatever he tells me next won't be the truth. Or if it is the truth, it'll only be a small part of the truth.

I know it. I just can't do anything about it.

"You're the kind of person I want on my team, Harlow," he says quietly. "We're older and wiser now. I think we can make a fellowship work for one year. Don't you?"

No, I don't think.

A lot can happen in a year. A lot *did* happen the last time we spent a year together.

And when it comes to him, I think I'm older and wiser, but it's not the kind of thing I want to test out any more than I want to test whether lake ice is solid enough for ice skating by driving a tank across it.

Some things just aren't a good idea. At all.

"Yes or no, Harlow?"

The correct answer is simple: *Thanks, but no.*

There's no way I can work with this man. I emerged from my last work experience with him battered, bruised and with a broken heart entirely of my own making. He has a unique and profound effect on me that other people do not possess. I *think* about him. His presence in a room makes my skin sizzle. I've never been able to control my reactions to him, and there's no reason to believe I'll be able to start now.

He's divorced now, Ally.

So? Who cares? His current marital status is absolutely none of my business and has zero effect on my life. He shut me down before. Ruthlessly, I might add. I'd be a fool not to learn from my past mistakes. I may be many things, but I always try not to be a fool when I can help it.

Thanks, but no.

I'm finally in a mature relationship. With Bruce. I need to focus. On *Bruce*. I can't scuttle my plans for my life just because this Dr. McDreamy wannabe reappears unexpectedly.

But...the Sphinx is a great doctor. An amazing teacher, hazing aside. He's got the wealth of knowledge and the willingness to share them. The most uncompromising expectations. The highest ethics. The best practices. The calmest demeanor. The most soothing and encouraging bedside manner. He is the platinum standard. Other docs I've worked with never measure up. They may have the knowledge, but it's locked inside their head because they lack the communication skills to be an effective teacher. Or they're so selfish and narcissistic that they don't even bother pretending to care that part of their job consists of instructing the next generation of surgeons. But not Dr. Jamison. He's got it all. Training with him is a huge privilege. The medical equivalent of a painter taking a personalized master class from Pablo Picasso.

If only I could shut off those blaring alarm bells in my head.

The problem is, they're right. There's plenty of reason for alarm here. This may be my dream opportunity, but the cost is too high. I can't do it. I shouldn't attempt to do it any more than a recovering alcoholic should attempt to work the graveyard shift at a bourbon distillery.

Why set yourself up for failure and, worse, disaster?

Thanks, but no.

Say it, Ally. Do the right thing.

"Harlow?" he says quietly.

"When do I start?" I ask.

Something palpable changes in him. It's not a smile

or a gasp of relief. Nothing like that. But the energy shifts in the room, and I could almost swear that it has something to do with his stern face and the secrets hidden behind his eyes.

"You can start— *Fuck*," he says, breaking off when his phone buzzes and he gets a glimpse of the display.

He gives me a triumphant look as he surges to his feet and heads for the door.

I know that look.

I *love* that look.

"What is it?" I ask, already breathless as I get up and hurry after him.

"You can scrub in with me right now. We've got an emergency. Let's go."

6

MICHAEL

"TREVOR?" I say three hours later. I lean over the bed and squeeze the IV'd arm of my patient, a drowsy nine-year-old with a sleep-smashed Afro and a heavily bandaged neck. "You with me, buddy?"

Trevor swats my hand away and frowns without opening his eyes. "Sleeping," he grumbles.

I exchange a quick and relieved grin with his mother, who's hunkered over the other side of the bed with Trevor's father.

And who's standing next to me? Ally.

I experience a high every time I come out of a successful surgery. And now? With Ally's assist and her presence at my right hand? That natural high is skimming the edge of euphoria.

"Wake up, Trev," I say, squeezing again. "I'm going to need proof of life before I let you go home to Mr. Peanut Butter."

Magic words. Trevor's lids fly open and he springs to life, yanking the cannula from his nose.

"It wasn't Mr. Peanut Butter's fault," he tells his

parents with the same urgency I'd expect him to demon-
strate if he were warning them about a house fire in the
middle of the night. "He didn't know what he was doing.
It was an accident. You can't get rid of him, okay?"

"I'm not getting rid of the dog. I'm getting rid of the
tug rope," his mother says darkly.

"Agreed," says Trevor's father, eyeballing the side of
his son's neck. "I just never thought a golden retriever
could do that kind of damage."

"Ah," I say, using my tablet to type a note in Trevor's
chart. "So you were able to adopt one of those elusive
toothless golden retrievers. Or was it a vegetarian golden
retriever that doesn't have the sharp teeth like other
dogs?"

"The doc's got jokes," Trevor's dad says, swapping a
sheepish grin with his wife.

"Those were actually halfway decent," Ally says with
an amused sidelong glance at me that makes my skin
hum with pleasure. "You should've heard what I had to
listen to in the OR. I can't decide what was worse. His
music choice or his jokes."

"Leave my peaceful piano music out of this," I tell
her, finishing with the tablet.

"*Peaceful piano*? Yeah, that's tragic," Trevor says to a
round of laughter. "Am I going to have a cool scar?" he
asks, touching his bandages as things quiet down. "Like
a vampire or something?"

"Don't get greedy," I say. "You're lucky to be alive. If
Mr. Peanut Butter had chomped on a little more neck
and a little less shoulder, this would be a whole different
story. Plus, I'm a fantastic plastic surgeon —"

"*Wow,*" Ally mutters.

"—and I don't get paid the big bucks to leave patients

looking like they were fed through a meat grinder. That said, vampires leave puncture wounds. Everyone knows that. So I'm guessing you'll look like you were attacked by a werewolf. If anything."

"Awesome," Trevor says happily as his parents roll their eyes. "When can I go home?"

"You rest. Eat something. We'll talk after that," I tell him, offering up a fist bump.

"Deal," he says.

"Thank you so much," Trevor's mother says, hurrying around the bed to meet Ally and me at the curtain. "We were scared to death."

There's just enough time for me to say, "That's what I'm here for," before she gives me the kind of thankful bear hug that is, I submit to you, every bit as gratifying as the big bucks I mentioned a minute ago.

"Thank you for taking such good care of Trevor," she says when she pulls back.

"Anytime. Not that I want to see Trevor again anytime soon," I say.

"Thanks, doc," says Trevor's dad, his handshake quickly escalating into another bear hug.

"*I* helped too," Ally says with exaggerated aggrievement.

"I didn't forget about you, Dr. Harlow," says Trevor's mom, quickly spreading some love Ally's way.

"I was just kidding," Ally says, laughing as she submits to this affection. I, meanwhile, watch the proceedings and try not to feel jealous of a hug—platonic or otherwise—that some other person is allowed to give Ally, but I am not. "Dr. Jamison did all the heavy lifting."

"I'm sure he couldn't have done it without you,"

Trevor's mother says as we duck out of their cubicle, and she's not wrong. Not exactly.

I mean, could I fix up the kid's neck by myself? Of course. Any day of the week, twice on Sundays and in my sleep.

But...

Would I feel so relaxed and content without Ally's intuitive presence in the OR, anticipating what I'm going to do and why I'm going to do it and then helping me get there before I need to ask? Would I feel so energized if I couldn't look up every now and then and see Ally's bright eyes shining at me over the top of her face mask?

No. I sure as hell would not.

What are you doing here, Jamison?

The voice in my head is an unwelcome intrusion into my day. I try to ignore it, but that's the thing about those little voices: there's no hiding from them. They don't go away.

What the hell do you think you're doing with Ally?

It's not like I have anything beyond a half-assed plan here. Or an end game.

I wanted more time with her, so I strategized a few moves and now I have a year with her. I wanted her closer, and now she's closer. Maybe too close. I'm sure my lawyers would give me a sternly worded warning about the dangers of lusting after employees if they knew the way my thoughts were running.

The big question now is: what next?

I frown as I take off my cap and hit the wall plate, some of my post-surgery high fading. The heavy metal doors swing open and we leave recovery. I want to ask her to dinner—it would feel so natural to ask her to dinner—but I don't dare. She's got a boyfriend. It's one thing to manipulate the situation and use my newfound wealth to engineer a job so she can work with me and (hopefully, eventually) hook up with me. But me asking her out when I know she has a boyfriend feels like a douchebag move.

I don't want to be that guy. I want to do the right thing. I'm just not sure I can.

So where am I with Ally? What now? How long can I realistically resist temptation?

No fucking idea.

"Nice job," she says as we drift over to the far end of the nurses' station and settle there.

"But of course," I say to get a rise out of her.

Sure enough, she scowls. My overactive imagination speculates that if we were together, she'd whack me. I'd grab her hand and keep it. Then I'd pull her in and steal a kiss or two—

"Give humility a chance sometimes," she says.

"Why?"

She laughs, a dazzling display of dimples, white teeth and sparkling eyes that strains my self-control to the breaking point, because I want to eat this woman alive. I want to swallow her whole. To inhale her. Absorb her. I want to touch her and imprint the feeling of every part of her body on every part of mine. Most of all, I want to stop keeping secrets and just tell her—for *once*—how fucking beautiful she is.

All the wanting knots up inside me, making my throat tight and my voice gruff.

"*You* did a good job," I tell her. "You've learned a couple of things."

"I can only hope," she says. "You'll have to tell me your surgeon origin story one of these days."

That's a new one on me. "My whatty-who?"

"Your *surgeon origin story*. What happened to make you want to be a surgeon? I've always wondered."

"Forget it," I say when the light bulb goes off over my head. "That's classified information."

"Oh, come on," she says, her expression brightening as she puts her hands in prayer position under her chin, her body all but quivering with excitement. "Now you *have* to tell me."

She's right. Because there's no way I can resist being the center of all this rapt attention. "This goes no further. I don't want the residents to start calling me the Sap instead of the Sphinx."

"Deal."

"There was this commercial for UNICEF or something, when I was about eight. A crying baby with a cleft palate from some Third World country. I had a cousin who was a baby at the time, so it hit me hard. Just this gut reaction. This alarm. How could that baby drink his bottle? What would happen to him? Who was going to do something? It was a whole thing. It became an obsession." Even now I feel the same visceral reaction and driving need to do what I can. "To my parents' credit, they indulged me. I think they thought I was crazy, but, on the other hand, who doesn't want their kid to grow up and be a doctor? So they got me all kinds of books and, I don't know, showed me documentaries and magazines and medical journals and stuff. I was amazed that someone could have a condition at birth or a grave injury in a car accident or from a dog bite and you could fix it. I mean, don't get me wrong, no one would sign up for this shit unless they were a stubborn Type A personality, but..."

It dawns on me that I've been talking for a long time, so I stop, feeling exposed. "Anyway. That's my origin story. Tell no one."

"No promises. Just know that I have the material I need to blackmail you at any time."

"Glad you asked?" I say, laughing.

"I *am* glad I asked." Her gaze is steady. Warm. Absolutely addictive. "There has to be something, you know? Unless a person is a complete psychopath, there's gotta be some reason he or she signs up for all the schooling. The exhaustion. The expense. The grueling work. The delayed gratification and sacrifice. I love what I do, but there were plenty of times when I thought about quitting. I'm not sure my friends or even my parents always understood why I did it."

"My ex-wife never understood," I say before I think to stop myself, and then it's out there: the hidden fault line buried deep beneath my marriage. The shaky foundation upon which it was built. In the sort of extremely personal information I'm not sure I've ever told anyone.

Ally's interest sharpens. I feel it.

"What do you mean?"

I shrug, struggling to put it into a few succinct words. "I mean, she thought I was crazy for being happy on five hours of sleep a night, if that, and no vacations and on-calls and nearly half a mill in student loan debt. She resented the fact that I had so little time with her. I don't blame her for that. She needs what she needs. And I need what I need. Two different things. No harm, no foul. We spent five years being unhappily married, but that's better than six years being unhappily married. But anyone who doesn't understand *that* about me doesn't understand *anything* about me. Period."

She nods thoughtfully, a vague frown marring her forehead.

Having reached the end of my impromptu soliloquy, I should shut the hell up. I want Ally and I to get to know each other better, but this is not the kind of thing I normally get into, and we're still at work. A place where boundaries are appropriate and required.

But I've got a couple more sentences that won't stay in my mouth.

"The thing is… The next time around, I plan to make sure my partner and I understand each other. Perfectly. It's important, don't you think?"

Maybe there's something a little too pointed about the way I'm looking at her, because she seems a little flustered as she hastily glances away.

"I *do* think," she says with a laugh that sounds a bit forced as she takes her cap off (these days, it's Van Gogh's sunflowers rather than Monet's water lilies) and reveals several curls that seem eager to escape from her bun. "I also think that you'll have plenty of candidates willing to test that theory with you. If you don't already."

I make a face, because this suggestion contains all the appeal of topping my morning cereal with grilled octopus slices.

"At this stage of my life, I'm into quality. Not quantity," I say, determined to steer this conversation back into normal waters before I freak one or both of us out. God knows I'm dangerously close to skirting that territory myself. "Come on. Let's hit the café and grab dinner before our bodies start to cannibalize themselves. I'll buy."

She blinks, coming out of an expression that's vaguely troubled. "You don't have to," she says.

Since I don't like the alternative, which is letting her go for the night and heading home to my expensive but lonely apartment for another long night of craving her, I *do* have to.

"It's the least I can do, since I'm not paying you yet," I say, trying to be a cool cat about it. "Plus, you eat yogurt. How expensive could that be?"

Grinning, she leads the way to the elevator and punches the button. "Keep it up and I'll order one of everything out of spite," she says sweetly.

"That's exactly the kind of pettiness I'd expect from you."

We're standing there laughing together in a moment that's destined to become one of the top three most delicious of my life when her phone buzzes. My heart sinks even before she pulls it out, because I know it's *him*. Bruce. Her fucking boyfriend. I know our moment is over and I'm not getting any dinner in the café. Worse, I know that *he* belongs with her and *I* don't.

She hesitates, her smile slowly drying up.

"Go ahead," I say dully. "Take it."

Nodding, she reaches into her pocket, extracts the phone and checks the display.

Naturally, I also check it.

Bruce, it says.

Fucker.

She glances back up at me, and I swear—I *swear*— she seems disappointed. Because the glow that lit her up a few seconds ago? No sign of it now.

"I should take this," she says as the phone buzzes again.

"Absolutely."

"Thanks for the dinner offer."

"No problem."

Luckily, the elevator arrives just then, giving me exactly the escape I need. I climb on, hit the button and turn to face the front, determined to keep my disappointment under wraps. This one lost dinner in a freaking hospital café is not the end of the world. It just feels like it.

"Have a great night, Harlow," I say.

She nods. The last thing I see before the elevator doors slide closed is the way she hesitates before answering the phone and raising it to her ear with something that looks like reluctance.

"MARGARITA NIGHT," I say with tremendous satisfaction as I join Kelly at her booth in the back the following night. I lean in for a hug and kiss before sliding into my seat and setting my phone on the table. "Have I mentioned that you're a freaking genius?"

"I had to think of some official occasion," she says, pointing to a large and frosty pomegranate margarita that she's thoughtfully ordered for me. "And whining that I'm bored and want a drink on a random Thursday night didn't seem to cut it."

"Agreed." I raise my glass, eager to begin the unwinding process after another long day in the OR. "Although I think we should call it frozen pomegranate margarita night. And that frees up other days of the week for, I don't know, frozen strawberry margarita night, traditional margarita on the rocks night, traditional margarita on the rocks with salt night and so on. Cheers."

"Cheers," she says, laughing. We clink and sip with appropriate gusto. "Thanks for coming on such short notice. I'm surprised I caught you before you went home and went for your jog or whatever you have on the schedule for tonight."

"Luckily, I went to the gym this morning."

"So it all worked out. This is a nice little bar, by the way. Good suggestion."

"It is," I say, succumbing to a pang of nostalgia as I look around. "The other interns and I used to come here all the time because it's so close to the hospital. We did a lot of bitching and unwinding here. It hasn't changed much."

I glance around, seeing the place through her fresh eyes. It's nothing fancy, but it's cozy and intimate and I love it. They serve coffee and pastries before noon, then segue into light bites, wine and cocktails with kick as the day wears on. Sometimes they bring in up-and-coming jazz bands. It feels like an old friend.

I have a lot of good memories here.

And one bad one.

Don't be a fool. Don't throw yourself at a man who will never feel the same way.

I feel my buoyant mood faltering and shove the memory far away. No need to wallow in the past. It's over and done. No good can come of it.

"So," Kelly says, resting her elbows on the table and leaning in with gleeful nosiness as she rubs her hands together. "What did the Sphinx want the other day? Tell me everything."

"You're not going to believe this. It was a job interview. He offered me a fellowship with him."

Kelly's smile vanishes. Her lower jaw drops and hovers just above the table for a long beat or two.

"What?"

"You heard me." I can barely contain my excitement. "You know he's starting his new practice, right? He wants me on the team. We have the same vision about working on cutting-edge practices. *And* he's paying me enough money to put a real dent in my student loans. I feel like I've won the lotto and found a pot of gold under my pillow."

She continues to gape.

"Stop being weird," I say as a ring of heat winds its way around my neck and begins its slow crawl north, to my cheekbones. The heavy note of defensiveness in my voice doesn't help matters any. "You don't look very happy for me."

"Of course I'm happy for you," she says, snapping out of it and trying to work up a passable smile. "It's just that I didn't see that coming."

"Neither did I."

She frowns thoughtfully, staring into the depths of her margarita. "So what made him hire *you*?"

"Hopefully, it's because I'm the kind of surgeon he wants on his team. Like he said when he hired me," I say, stung.

"Of *course* you are," she says, rolling her eyes. "Don't go getting your panties in a bunch. You're a great doctor. Anyone would be lucky to have you. It's just… You've been talking this whole time about how hard it is to land a fellowship. Especially in plastics. And you just had this casual interview? You didn't have to submit your résumé or anything? Or meet his partners? I'm not saying any of that is a bad thing, but…isn't that unusual?"

I shrug, trying to look unconcerned and not at all as though I've been asking myself the same questions on an endless loop. But she's right: I'm a highly competent doctor, but no one's counting on me to light the world on fire with my groundbreaking surgical techniques. Besides that, fellowships don't just land in people's laps. Plenty of other doctors who are still looking have better credentials than mine. And I'm betting that none of them hit the same speed bumps during their residency that I did and needed a leave of absence.

Why did he hire you, Ally?

Why did he hire you?

I tell her the same thing that I've been telling myself:

"It may be a little unusual, but we've worked together before. He already knows me and knows that we have similar work ethics and styles because he trained me. I'm a known quantity. He probably wants to save himself from a whole big search and hiring process. Why reinvent the wheel? Plus, we're both interested in new techniques for skin grafting and stuff like that. So we share the same vision, like I said. And this is the biggie—he's got the money and resources to do whatever he wants to do with his practice. He doesn't have to jump through any hoops he doesn't want to."

"That makes sense," she says, her expression clearing.

"Anyway, I'm not looking a gift horse in the mouth. I'm not stupid. What the hell do I care why he hired me as long as I'm hired?"

"Amen to that, sister," she says fervently, offering a fist bump.

"His reasons for hiring me are none of my business," I say, raising my glass to her before sipping again.

"My only concern is that—"

"Oh my *God*," I say, letting my exasperation run free. "Here you go again."

"—I thought you were planning to stay away from him. Are you *sure* this is a good idea?"

Isn't that the million-dollar question?

Keeping my expression neutral feels like standing on the sidewalk and hoisting a grand piano to a third-floor apartment all by myself. Let's just say that it takes an unnatural feat of strength.

"It's fine," I say as airily as I can manage.

"Yeah, but how fine could it be? You used to be obsessed with the guy. I feel like you're playing with fire."

Like I need a reminder. Especially when the conversation he and I had after surgery the other day is still so fresh in my mind. I've been replaying it in my mind, with the relentless focus of a tween binge-watching every episode of *Pretty Little Liars*.

I've always wondered about his wife. Ex-wife now. Her looks. Her personality. Whether they were a good fit or not. Now I know.

They were not.

Not that this fascinating information has anything to do with me and my life. That's the thing I need to keep in mind.

"Would you kindly give it a rest?" I say. "Can't I just enjoy my good news for ten minutes without your doomsday predictions?"

"*No*. As your best friend, it's my job to tell you the truth. No matter what."

"Fine," I say, snatching up the menu and flipping it open. "Consider yourself demoted for the night. We're...

friendly acquaintances. Now can I enjoy my drink in peace? And what about nachos? I feel like we need some nachos."

"Oh, we definitely need nachos," she says, also opening her menu. "Just don't say I didn't warn you."

"Whatever. Do we want standard chips with guac or do we want to go all in?"

"I'm all in, baby."

"Music to my ears," I say, shutting my menu with a decisive snap and looking around for the server. No sign of him or her, alas. "So how are things going with you this week? How'd your date go with—"

My phone lights up and buzzes. I give it a passing glance—it's Bruce; I can always call him back later—and refocus on Kelly.

"Sorry," I say. "Tell me everything about your date with the guy you met in the bagel shop."

"It's okay," she says quickly, flapping a hand. "It's *Bruce*. Answer it."

"It's not a big deal."

"What is wrong with you?" Shooting me one of those scathing looks that the hostess always gives you when you try to sneak into the latest hot restaurant without a reservation, she snatches the phone up and hits the button. "Hey, Bruce. How are you? We're just grabbing drinks. Hang on."

I watch her with a vague feeling of annoyance as she props the phone against the wall so we can both see the screen. Bruce and I text each other throughout the day, and we'll have our standard bedtime video chat later. I just don't see any need to speak to him again *now*, in the middle of our girls' night.

"Okay, Bruce," she says. "Can you hear us okay?"

"I can. Hey, babe," he says with a warm smile just for me as I ease within camera range. I see that he's lounging in his D.C. apartment and deep into his post-work routine, which includes his sofa, a white T-shirt, an open bottle of craft beer with several empties on the coffee table and, probably, ESPN. Let's just say he's a creature of habit. "How's your day been?"

"I can't complain. Especially now that I have a margarita," I say.

"What's this I hear about you moving to the city, Bruce?" Kelly says. "That's exciting news."

"I think so. It's not a done deal. I still need to interview for the position. But fingers crossed it works out. This long-distance thing isn't working for me. Too many lonely nights."

"Aww," Kelly says, dividing a dewy-eyed look between us as though she's the bride's mother watching her baby glide down the aisle toward the altar. "I'm so happy for you two. You're such a sweetie, Bruce. Note to self: find someone who looks at me the way Bruce looks at Ally."

Bruce laughs, but I shift uncomfortably. "Knock it off," I tell Kelly. "You're going to drive Bruce off with all your sappy talk."

"Not a chance," Bruce says.

Something about his open adoration makes me feel flushed, irritable and vaguely out of sorts. Like I've spent too much time out on the beach with the sun beating down on my head and need to make my escape as soon as possible.

"Let me call you when I get home," I tell him. "Kelly

and I are going to order something to eat. And I need to catch up on every gruesome detail of her personal life."

"Sounds good," he says.

"Is it your weekend to come to New York, Bruce?" Kelly asks.

"I wish," he says. "But I've got my cousin's wedding. I couldn't weasel out of it."

"You're not going down for that?" Kelly asks me, staying true to form and never missing the chance to put me in the hot seat.

"I'm not," I say cheerily, giving her a veiled *drop it* look as best I can.

"It's not for lack of an invitation," Bruce says with an exaggerated frown for my benefit.

I shift again, realize I'm coming perilously close to fidgeting and force myself to sit still. "I'm on call and I've got some things I need to do around my apartment. Like catch up on sleep," I say, trying to infuse my voice with a modicum of regret.

But the truth is, I regret nothing.

First of all, the whole back-and-forth thing on top of my long hours at the hospital is getting to be a bit of a grind. A break this weekend sounds like a small slice of heaven. Second, and I would take a sledgehammer to the knee before admitting this to Bruce, I find his huge and boisterous family exhausting and best experienced in small doses. Very small. As someone who comes from a quiet family of four, I'm not used to either the decibel level or their propensity to argue every point—including every single freaking political point—as though the penalty for agreement or compromise is immediate execution by backyard firing squad.

"I'll be in town next weekend, Kel," Bruce says. "Maybe I'll see you then."

"Sounds good," Kelly says, waving. "See you soon."

"Bye, Kelly," he says before turning back to me. "Bye, babe. Love you."

"Bye," I say, waving.

Keenly aware of Kelly's speculative gaze on my face, I can't hang up fast enough. Although a smarter woman surely would've prolonged the call just so she wouldn't have to endure the questioning that's about to come her way.

"What's that about?" she asks with the intensity of Annalise Keating grilling a witness on the stand in open court. "He says *I love you* and you say *bye*?"

See? What did I tell you?

I take a big gulp of my margarita before answering. I need it at this point. My nerves feel fried.

"Okay, first of all, he didn't say *I love you*. He said *love you*. There's a difference. He says *love you* every time he hangs up from talking with anyone. That *love you* was probably aimed at you as well."

"He wasn't looking at me when he said it," she says, eyes narrowed.

"And second," I continue loudly, "that's not a word that should just get thrown around."

"Maybe he's not just throwing it around, Ally. Especially considering he's talking about moving here to be with you."

"You are just on a tear tonight, aren't you?" I say, trying to laugh it off as I reach for my drink again. "Can we order our loaded nachos now? Is that allowed?"

"*Me?* I don't know what's going on with *you*—"

"Harlow," comes a deep voice as a figure looms over the table. "Fancy meeting you here."

Startled, we glance around and discover none other than the Sphinx himself toting a carry-out bag. My heart begins a frantic sprint toward cardiac arrest, and that's *before* I take a good look at him. Meanwhile, Kelly's breath hitches with subtle but unmistakable feminine appreciation, which tells me that she's seeing what I'm seeing.

Allow me to paint the picture for you.

Aviator shades. Wet hair. Sweat-ringed T-shirt. Knit shorts. Shoulders. Arms. Legs. Muscles. Clean sweat.

Basically the human version of Zeus.

This, right here, is one of the most troublesome things about Dr. Jamison: he's always sexy and getting sexier. In scrubs. In scrubs with his lab coat. In a suit. In running shorts. If I ever have the misfortune of seeing him in swimming trunks, I'll probably turn multi-orgasmic on the spot.

"Dr. Jamison," I say once my hormonal surge recedes to a manageable level. "You didn't mention you were training for the Olympics."

"Nothing like that," he says, laughing as he turns to Kelly. "Just a jog around the park and a quick dinner before I go back to work. Michael Jamison. And you are…?"

All things considered, Kelly recovers pretty quickly for someone whose eyes have been replaced with puffy red hearts. "Kelly Henderson," she says, offering her hand and a glorious smile.

"Ah. The famous Kelly. I've heard good things." He shoots me a quick look before hastily wiping his free hand on the dry part of his T-shirt and shaking Kelly's hand. "Sorry. I'm a mess."

Yep, I think glumly. He's exactly the kind of sweaty mess a woman wants between her legs and pressing her deep into the mattress for the fucking of a lifetime.

"You're going back to the hospital?" I ask.

"Back to the office, actually," he says with a rueful smile. "Paperwork. But at least I get my loaded nachos. I had a taste for them. I want to make sure they're as good as I remember."

I try not to attach any significance to the fact that he also likes loaded nachos. Everyone likes loaded nachos.

On the other hand, *he* jogs. *I* jog.

Not everyone jogs.

Take Bruce, for instance.

"You should go home. Rest. You've been in surgery all day," I tell him, trying to keep my simmering obsession with him at bay.

"Eh. Home is a little too quiet these days." He says it with the air of someone determined to be upbeat about his circumstances, but there's no missing the veiled sadness and loneliness. Something about his melancholy mood—there's a word I don't use every day: *melancholy*—touches me. More than that, it makes my heart ache. For reasons I am determined not to explore. "Looks like I'm interrupting margarita night. I'll get out of here and leave you to it. Before the manager comes over and kicks me out because of my farm animal smell."

"I would've characterized it as more of a smoked gym bag smell," I say, now too flustered to look him in the eye as I hastily reach for my drink to give myself something to do. "But anyway. Have a great night."

"You too, Harlow," he says, laughing again.

God.

That husky, deep-throated sound does me in every time. It's like an endless shiver over my skin that awakens hidden nerve endings all up and down my body.

He lingers as though there's something else he wants to say.

I keep drinking, afraid to do anything else. Especially look at him.

And all I can think is how unfair this situation is.

Look, I know I shouldn't have taken the job with him. I know I'm wildly attracted to him. But I'm trying to do the right thing here. I'm minding my own business, trying to have a drink with my BFF before going home to video-chat with my boyfriend. A great guy who's willing to move to NYC to be with me. I didn't *ask* for Dr. Jamison to show up like *that* and scramble my sensitive female circuits. But he did. And now I feel like my thoughts and all my best intentions have been poisoned. I feel as though he keeps throwing pebbles in my pond and making far-reaching ripples where there should be none.

Worst of all, I have no idea what to do about my situation.

No fucking idea at all.

I just know that this is all a million times harder than I thought it would be.

"Well," he finally says, giving up on me and turning to Kelly. "Great meeting you."

"You too," she says.

He walks off.

I lower my empty glass to the table and make a production out of straightening my napkin, awaiting Kelly's reaction with dread.

"*That's* the Sphinx?" she asks, more than a little breathless.

"That's him," I say grimly.

"Oh my God." She reaches around for her purse, gets up, slings it over her shoulder and turns toward the bathroom, still looking dazed. "Oh my *God*."

Exactly.

She walks off, but not before muttering two words I really wish I could un-hear.

"Poor Bruce."

8

MICHAEL

"I DON'T KNOW what your fascination is with hospi-
tals," I say several days later as my twin sister and I
continue our leisurely circuit of the nurses' station and
head toward the double doors leading to the atrium.
"Most people try to avoid them."

Mia frowns at me. "I am allowed to take an interest
in your life and see where you work. Especially when
you get a great new office suite."

"That's fair," I say. "But you've already seen my new
office. Why can't we go to lunch like normal people?
Why do we have to make this detour through the ER?"

"Because it makes me feel like I'm in an episode of
Grey's Anatomy," she says happily, looking around for any
sign of action. The place is crowded and busy, but it's a
controlled chaos. The way we like to keep it. "I keep
waiting for some EMTs to burst through the double
doors with a doctor straddling a patient on a stretcher.
And then the doctor could frantically give the patient
chest compressions while they're on their way to the OR.

Maybe they'd get the paddles out and yell *clear!* I want to see it all go down."

I snort. "You realize that things aren't usually that dramatic, don't you? And that your whole scenario would mean some poor patient was close to death?"

She makes a dismissive sound. "No actual patients were harmed in the making of the scenario, I'll have you know. You'll swoop in and save everyone's life. The patient will be home by dinner."

"Good to know," I say, choking back a laugh. "I thought you were going to say you're hoping to see McDreamy or McSteamy."

"I have my own sexy doctor now, thanks," she says smugly, waving her diamond-heavy left hand in my face.

I'd like to scowl, but I can't quite manage it. Not when she's aglow with contentment over her recent reconciliation and engagement with one of my best friends, Liam, who was also her long-lost college love.

"How could I forget? It's been two whole seconds since you mentioned it," I say.

"Well, that's how you are. It's always all about *you*, isn't it?"

We laugh.

"You just remember who's responsible for your newfound happiness," I say.

"My sexy fiancé Liam?"

"No. *Me*. If I hadn't played eleventh-hour match-maker to you two knuckleheads, you'd probably be rolled up in the fetal position somewhere right now, crying your eyes out. You both would."

"That's sadly true," she says.

"I know."

"Oh, whatever. I'm starting to get hungry, so we need

to focus. Where should we go for lunch? I'm thinking sushi."

"Hang on," I say, distracted by the sight of a familiar scrub-wearing figure with sandy curls and a spectacular ass emerging from a cubicle up ahead and speaking with one of the techs. My heart pumps pleasantly faster, as though someone has shifted my transmission up a gear or two.

"Or I could go for tacos," Mia adds, but I'm no longer listening.

"Harlow," I call.

Ally pauses and looks around as she swings her stethoscope around her neck. She sees me and goes very still before reaching up to smooth her hair, which is exactly the sort of body language that keeps me on high alert these days.

The air prickles when we're around each other. I refuse to believe that I'm the only one who feels it.

Especially when her face brightens—exactly like *that* —every time I show up.

I head her way, not really caring whether my sister tags along. Nor do I particularly care that my sister, who roots for information about my personal life the way raccoons root for dumpster food outside restaurants every night, will get kindling for her eternal fire to get me happily settled with the right woman. I haven't seen much of Ally since the other night at the bar, and I don't intend to let this opportunity pass.

"Dr. Jamison," Ally says, her attention swinging between me and Mia. "How are you?"

"What brings you down here?" I ask.

"A seven-year-old and his bike decided to take on a tree," she says with a rueful smile. "The tree won, in case you were wondering. I did what I could, but she's going to have a Harry Potter scar. I'm guessing this is your sister?"

"It is," I say, excruciatingly aware of Mia's rapt attention as I reach out and draw her closer. I know that there's nothing going on between me and Ally. Yet. I also know that I'm making a grave tactical error by revealing even the smallest hint of my feelings to my nosy sister, who still needles me about some girl I kissed after school in the fifth grade. But there's something immensely satisfying about bringing these two women together and seeing what happens. Something that feels...important. "How did you know?"

"Because I'm exceptionally observant and clever," Ally tells me, one delicate brow arched. "And also because she looks like God said, 'Give me another Michael Jamison, but make it female this time.'" She turns to Mia and extends her hand. "Ally Harlow. Great to meet you."

"Great to meet *you*," Mia says as they shake. Her entire demeanor is perked and alert as she watches Ally, like a golden retriever whose owner has opened the treat jar. "Do you work with Michael?"

"I actually work *for* him," Ally says. "Again. He was my chief resident years ago. Now he's my boss."

"You poor thing," Mia says with an exaggerated shudder and grimace.

"Poor, my ass," I say. "I taught Harlow everything she knows."

"Not *everything*, because *I*, unlike *you*, actually know how to be humble," Ally says acidly.

We all laugh together. It feels good.

"I wasn't going to say anything, because you seem

like such a nice person," Ally says, adopting a grave tone as she eases closer to Mia. "But you know he's a monster, right? I've still got the PTSD to prove it. He wasn't happy unless he made at least one intern cry every shift. Usually more."

I can't control a bark of laughter at this unlikely image. Ally? I'm positive that if they ran her down to the x-ray department and took a few scans, they'd discover that her spine is made of titanium.

"No one can make *you* cry, Harlow. Not for lack of trying," I say darkly.

"See? What did I tell you?" Ally tells Mia. "A *monster*."

We all laugh again.

"Sorry about that," Mia says. "My parents and I did the best we could with him."

"I'm sure you tried," Ally says. "Don't blame yourself."

"But you're subjecting yourself to his reign of terror again?" Mia asks. "You must be a glutton for punishment, Ally."

"Or just dumber than the average bear," Ally says.

Maybe my healthy ego is leading me astray, but I'm ready to swear on a stack of Bibles if necessary that I hear a trace of wistfulness in her voice. I also notice that she doesn't look me or my sister in the eye when she says it.

"Godspeed," Mia says with more enthusiasm than I think is strictly necessary. "Don't let him run you ragged."

"I won't," Ally says. But her smile seems strained and she's still having difficulties with eye contact. She plows ahead anyway. "You should make your brother take you to lunch while you're here. And not lunch in the café, either. There's a great Greek place around the corner. Also a taco place."

"*Tacos*. I like how you think, Ally. You should come with us." Mia shoots a pointed glance in my direction. "I assume you allow her to have a lunch break, Michael?"

"Absolutely," I say quickly, grateful for any kind of help I can get in my quest to make headway with Ally. If my sister wants to help, I'm happy to have her on board. "You should come, Harlow."

Ally's gaze connects with mine just long enough to give me a hint of her ambivalence and to generate another crackling field of electricity between us that makes the hair on my nape and arms stand at attention.

"Thanks, but I can't," she says with an unmistakable tinge of regret. "I've got a couple of patients I need to check on. Plus I need to— *Oh, what a gorgeous diamond, Mia! Are you engaged?*"

Mia immediately lapses into blushing bride mode, all smiles and glowing happiness as she extends her hand to give Ally a good look at the ring. "I am. My fiancé Liam went to school with me and Michael back at NYU. We recently reconnected after a bad breakup and spending all this time apart."

"Oh, yeah?" Ally says, brimming with bright interest. "Sounds like there's a story there. How much time apart?"

"Twelve years," Mia says.

"Twelve years! And you just picked up right where you left off?"

"More or less." Mia hesitates. "Don't get me wrong, it was bumpy for a minute. And we had some growing up to do. But he was the right guy for me back then, and he's still the right guy for me now. That didn't change. It will never change. Part of me has always known that. And that's probably way more than you needed to hear about a perfect stranger."

"No, it's fine," Ally says. "That's a great story. Best wishes to both of you."

"What about *you*, Ally?" Mia asks, her nosiness trajectory headed straight for the top. "Married? Engaged?"

"Ah, no." Ally pauses, then clears her throat and backs up a step, giving the sudden impression that she'd rather be anywhere on earth—including the rim of a rumbling volcano—than here having this conversation. "Boyfriend. Well. Don't let me keep you from your lunch—"

"Nice," Mia says. "Should we be listening for wedding bells for the two of you?"

I wait, my entire body attuned to any nuances of the response Ally's about to give. Basically like a giant ear.

"Oh, no," Ally says quickly. "It's way too soon for anything like that."

"I see," Mia says with something that looks like grim satisfaction. Although I have no idea why. Not engaged could turn into engaged in the blink of an eye, as Mia and Liam recently demonstrated. "Well, best wishes to you and…?"

"Bruce," Ally supplies.

"Best wishes to you and Bruce," Mia says.

"Thanks," Ally says, but her smile seems fragile as she turns to go, as though the arrangement of her lips, teeth and dimples is a house of cards susceptible to the slightest bump. "I'd better check on those patients. Enjoy your lunch."

My sister barely waits until Ally heads for another cubicle before turning to me.

"That's *her*, isn't it?" she says with the fervor of a manic Elvis fan who thinks she's spotted the King hanging around a Vegas casino. "The woman you like? The one you used to work with back when you were married? I could tell by the way you looked at her."

There's only one appropriate answer when my sister gets like this. If I don't shut down this inquisition right now, I'll find myself strapped in and stretched out on a rack with her hand on the crank before dinnertime.

"I have no idea what you're talking about. Should we hit up the taco place?"

"Because she's not in love with her boyfriend," she says urgently. "You get that, don't you?"

I falter, breaking cover as a cool cat because I *don't* know that, and I could use Mia's insight here if she has any.

"Excuse me?" I say with the little nonchalance I can muster.

"You're such an *idiot*," she says, smacking my shoulder for emphasis. I'd prefer not to be physically abused by my sister in front of my work colleagues, but I'm willing to make the sacrifice if it helps me get Ally. "Did you hear her answer about her boyfriend just now? She doesn't want to marry *him*. She's not in love with *him*. If she were, she'd giggle and say something like 'it's early days yet' or 'don't jinx me.' She wouldn't act like I'd suggested she marry her first cousin."

I frown, staring at the cubicle Ally disappeared into. Is that true? Could Mia be right?

"You know I'm right," Mia says, following my line of sight. "Don't screw this up. You've been divorced long enough to know that the dating world sucks. And I really like Ally. She's warm and sweet and funny. Not like Patricia, who was cold, aloof and bitchy. Ally is a good match for you and your strong and silent façade."

"My *what*?" I say, trying to decide whether to be offended.

"She's way better than Patricia ever was," she continues. "Don't act like you don't know what I'm talking about."

I repress a cringe as I think about my ex. She was a blond and blue-eyed Charlize Theron type, meaning that she was drop-dead gorgeous. Unfortunately, she had all the human warmth and compassion of a marble statue dipped in concrete, as I've mentioned. Something I probably would have noticed sooner if I'd been older and not so enamored of her looks.

She was no Ally. That's for damn sure.

"You need Ally in your life," my sister adds, now staring me down. "You know you do. Don't pretend you don't."

Pretend. Huh. Yeah. I'm sick of pretending that I don't have feelings for Ally. Sick of trying to be the good guy here. Sick of not knowing whether the things I experience with her are all in my head or whether she feels them to.

I don't know where things are going between me and Ally. I just know that they can't stay where they are.

Not if I want to stay sane.

In a sign of my growing turmoil, I drop the act with my sister. Hell, I've got nothing to lose. Neither one of us believes my routine anyway.

"I want her to be happy. If she's happy with him, then I'm happy for her. I'm not trying to disrupt her life,"

I say. "I'm just coming off a divorce. I've got nothing to offer her. She deserves someone who's all in. Someone that's not me."

Mia hits me with one of those looks that's full of smiling eyes, bottomless empathy and support.

"It's up to Ally to decide who she needs in her life, choirboy." She squeezes my arm. I find the unexpected touch surprisingly comforting. "If she's got everything she needs with her boyfriend, then there's no opening for you to disrupt anything. Is there? And if it were me, I'd want to know I had a chance to explore a connection with a great guy like you before taking things too far with some other guy. I imagine she's attracted to you, if nothing else. Anyone would be."

I can't stop thinking about you. I can't stop wanting your hands on my body...

The cherished memory from that long-ago night in the bar pops into my head from nowhere. The words combine with my sister's wisdom to hit me hard. Hard enough to make answering difficult. There's nothing I wouldn't do or give to hear Ally say she still has feelings for me. The thought that I've squandered my one and only chance with her is killing me.

"She was into me once," I tell Mia. "Maybe she isn't now."

"Maybe she is."

Yeah, maybe she is. That's what my instinct keeps telling me. Too bad inertia has me pinned in place. Inertia and fear. It's so much easier to live with the fantasy hope that there's something there between us rather than risk her shooting me down and smashing my tender and longstanding feelings against the rocks.

What would I do then? No fucking idea. I'm positive

that the disappointment would leave me gutted. As a guy who's endured the pain of a divorce, I'd really like to hope that I've endured my share of heartache for the foreseeable future.

But you just never know.

"Maybe I'm too chickenshit to find out," I say, my ears burning.

"I doubt that."

"That makes one of us," I mutter, folding my arms and shifting uncomfortably because I find it impossible to look her in the eye when I'm supposed to be strong and confident no matter what.

She seems to understand, which is one of the best things about having a twin. They understand everything, especially the things you can't say.

"You'll get it figured out. Meanwhile, I'm going to the restroom. When I get back, I demand tacos, because I'm starving. Got it?" she says.

"Got it," I say, cracking a smile.

"Be right back."

She takes off just as Ally emerges from her cubicle and heads for a nearby computer stand. Acting on impulse, I join her as she's typing something up. I'd love to claim that I have some grand scheme worked out to make my big move, but the truth is much simpler than that.

If she's in the room, I want to be with her. Close enough to see the sparkle in her eyes and whiff the scent of vanilla on her skin. Twenty feet away isn't good enough.

"I'm pretty sure my sister's going to cancel lunch if you can't come with us," I say, leaning against the wall next to her. "Thanks for that."

She represses a smile as she continues typing. "What can I say? I have that effect on people."

She certainly does.

"So. Big plans for the weekend?" It belatedly occurs to me that the question tiptoes dangerously close to personal territory, so I add a tiny embellishment. "I'm thinking of having everyone from the office over for drinks or some such. Esprit de corps and all that."

She stops typing and glances at me, one brow hiked up. "What do *you* know about esprit de corps?"

"More than you'd suspect. It's the sort of thing bosses are supposed to do."

"If you say so," she says, not bothering to hide her ongoing incredulity.

"Maybe early Saturday evening?"

Something in her expression closes off as she returns to typing. "That sounds great. You should totally do it. But I can't come."

"Oh." The news that I probably won't see her over the weekend—and it's not even a long holiday weekend, just a standard two-day weekend—kicks off an irrational wave of disappointment. I shove my hands in my pockets because that's a better option than, say, using them to punch this wall or flip over her computer stand. "Off to D.C.?"

"Nope." Maybe I'm imagining things, but I detect a new tightness in her voice. "Bruce is coming here. We're looking at apartments."

Fuuuuck.

I stand there and try to absorb this information, doing my best impersonation of a man pretending he's not being stabbed with an ice pick through the rib cage.

"Apartments." I clear my throat, nod and plaster on

the face I'd use if she told me she won a free dinner for two. "That's great. So it's a done deal, then? Him moving here?"

"Not yet. We're just getting the lay of the land."

Part of me wants to leave it at that and slink away to lick my wounds over a multi-margarita lunch with my sister. Another, louder, part of me demands that I do something I have thus far avoided and grow a pair of freaking balls.

So I stay right where I am and force my voice to work again.

"Excited?"

She finishes typing, gives the mouse a decisive final click and meets my gaze again. There's something steely about her jaw that wasn't there before.

"Of course I'm excited," she says, eyes glittering as she shrugs and gives me a smile that stops when it reaches the halfway point. "This is what I've always wanted. A great guy. A home. A partner. A *life*. What kind of fool wouldn't be excited, Dr. Jamison?"

And there it is. All the answer I need, whether I like it or not.

If she's happy, I'm happy.

"Good for you, Harlow," I say, wanting to mean it and hating myself because I don't. Luckily, my sister reappears just then, giving me the out I need. "I'll have people over some other weekend. And you can bring Bruce."

"Great. Thanks."

She turns and heads away from me, leaving me watching as she goes. She passes a patient room just as a youngish voice shouts with excitement.

"The cafeteria's this way, Jacob!"

That's all the warning she gets before two boys—they look like they're about nine or ten—race out of the room and plow directly into her. She yelps as she hits the floor hard at my feet.

I, meanwhile, undergo an eerie out-of-body experience that catapults me back to another day in the ER.

Her sudden absolute stillness as she lies there, facedown and unconscious, is forever seared into my brain. Never in my life, before or since, have I felt that sort of cataclysmic terror.

Something comes over me. Alarm. Blind rage. A raging case of PTSD. I can't explain it other than to say that I've been down this road before with Ally being injured in an emergency room mishap. And the sight of someone potentially injuring her again makes me lose my fucking mind.

"Watch what you're doing!" I roar at the kids, who already look stricken. "This is not a playground!"

"We're sorry!" one of them cries. "We didn't mean to knock her down! We're really sorry!"

But I don't have time for those kids. I'm too busy squatting beside Ally as she levers up to her elbows.

"I'm okay," she says with an embarrassed laugh. "Nothing to see here, folks."

"Don't move," I bark, reaching for her. "Let me check your head."

"We're really sorry! We didn't mean to—"

"I'm fine," she says, smacking my hands away as she surges to her feet without difficulty. "I didn't even hit my head."

"I'll just take a look," I say, in no mood to take anyone's word for it that she's okay. I whip out my flashlight with every intention of checking her pupils and then paging neuro for a consult just to be sure. Maybe ordering a CT scan. But a new interruption arrives as the apparent dad of the two hooligans races out of the room and surveys the scene.

"Jacob? Andy?" he says, scooping his boys closer and eyeballing me and Ally. "What the hell did you do?"

"It's okay," Ally says quickly, flashing a reassuring smile. "Just a little accident—"

"Which wouldn't have happened if you'd kept a better eye on your kids, buddy," I say, some runaway protective instinct propelling me to edge in front of her, lest these kids get any more funny ideas. "This isn't a school gym."

"Dr. Jamison," she says sharply, squeezing my arm and giving me sidelong warning look that has sparks shooting out of it. "I'm *fine*. It was an *accident*."

Then she edges past *me* and says a few further words to the dad and kids, but I don't catch them. I'm too busy realizing that my booming voice has caused more than a few heads to turn in my direction. Including my sister's. Judging by her shocked expression, she made her untimely return from the bathroom at the exact moment I started ranting like a lunatic about a nonevent.

But tell that to my racing heart.

"What the hell was *that* about?" Ally cries, rounding on me the second the dad and kids head in the cafeteria's direction.

"You *sure* you're okay?" I ask, giving her a once-over and reaching for my flashlight again. I'd feel much better if she let me check her pupils—

"Yes, I'm sure," she says, incredulous. "Why are you acting like a maniac?"

More heads turn in our direction, but fuck it, I don't care. I'm trying to do the right thing here. I'm trying to be a good guy. I'm trying not to lose my fucking head. But maybe it's way past too late for all that.

And she just scared the shit out of me.

"Maybe because I don't want to spend another night of my life wondering if you're seriously injured or not, Ally," I snarl, relishing her startled look as I loom over her. "*That's* why."

She stiffens and gapes at me. I can't tell whether it's because of my tone or because of my first-ever use of her first name, and I don't care either way.

I just know that I can't—I literally *cannot*—keep pretending that this woman is a standard hospital colleague to me.

"Let's go," I snap at my sister when the prickling tension between Ally and me becomes overwhelming. "I don't know what a guy has to do to get a taco around here."

As I walk off, I catch Ally and Mia exchanging a bewildered look out of the corner of my eye. I ignore it.

The same way I'm determined to ignore my roiling emotions and the memories of that harrowing night with Ally.

9

MICHAEL

BUT THAT'S the thing about memories, isn't it? They
stubbornly refuse all our efforts to sink them to the
bottom of our consciousness. They rise, like dead bodies
floating to the surface of a lake, much to the dismay of
the unlucky murderer.

Don't think about it, moron, I tell myself that evening as
I throw on my workout gear and hit the crowded park
for what I hope will be a head-clearing run. And I *don't*
think about it. For thirty good seconds, while I pick up
the pace, start pumping my arms and find my rhythm, I
notice things that have nothing to do with Ally Harlow.
Like the unexpected crispness of the breeze as it ripples
through the leaves and across my skin. And the number
of Frisbee-catching golden retrievers visible at a single
glance—three. Hell, I even decide it might be nice to
stop by the bar for a drink and maybe some nachos and
chicken fingers on the way home. God knows I'm not
going to cook myself dinner in my high-end but woefully
underused kitchen. For thirty whole seconds, I solidify
my plans for the evening.

And then…

"What's the issue, Harlow?"

"It's nothing."

I brush her away once. Maybe even twice. But she keeps coming. That's one of the most infuriating things about Ally. Her ruthless persistence when it comes to commandeering every thought in my head. She's never happy until she blocks out every other freaking thing in my life.

I see everything that happened that night with the same immediacy and clarity that I'm seeing a teenager rollerblade up ahead of me right now.

I round a corner in the ER and come upon Ally standing outside a room looking lost and forlorn, like an abandoned duckling. She watches as they wheel out a crash cart. As a couple more people file out of the room, including Dr. Smith from neuro, who grimly heads to the waiting area, probably to notify the family. As they wheel out a sheet-covered body and head for the service elevator that runs down to the morgue. I note the paleness of her face and her shell-shocked expression. I'm not close enough to see her chin trembling, but I bet it is.

I've seen this movie before, from beginning to tragic end. I've lived this movie myself. It's the story of life for surgical interns working in level I trauma centers. She had a patient. She didn't expect the patient to die. The patient thoughtlessly died anyway. Now Ally is grappling with all sorts of hairy life-and-death questions, and probably also questioning her own skills, when the bottom line is simple: even when you're at the top of your game, you can't save everyone. People are going to die sometimes. For no good reason.

Nothing you can do about it. Life as a surgeon, folks.

I absorb the entire scene and quickly lapse into an existential crisis right there in the ER. Ally's upset is not my problem. She's not on my service today. I've got my own shit to deal with. I came down to the ER to consult on a motorcycle accident patient with a nasty scalp laceration. That's my priority.

More importantly, I'm a married guy who knows that he's way too attracted to some other woman. I've got an issue with Ally. She's an open jar of honey and I'm a hungry bear. That being the case, it's important for me to avoid her whenever possible. To keep all the appropriate barriers up and reinforced so I don't get myself jammed up. Which is exactly what I'd expect my wife to do if she found herself in my situation. Ally equals temptation. It's an easy problem to solve. We're not talking organic chemistry here.

Funny thing, though: temptation is a lot easier to resist when you avoid it the way you avoid vampires after dark or werewolves during the full moon.

And Ally looks as though she's close to tears. She never cries. I've rarely even seen her frazzled, which makes this so startling and compelling.

Ally's really in pain. She needs someone. I need to be the someone.

I hesitate, drowning in ambivalence.

The tension between my wife and me lately has been so thick that I wonder if she'd even care if I, say, registered for an online dating site or got myself hit by a speeding bus.

And my patient is unlikely to die in the next five minutes without my input on how many staples he needs to fix his noggin. The dumbass is lucky to be alive. He should've been wearing a helmet.

So I round the nurses' station and head straight for Ally.

Which was, I suppose, always a foregone conclusion.

"Hey," I say, startling her.

"Dr. Jamison." She hastily ducks her head and wipes her eyes. "Hey."

I give her a second to collect herself and pretend I don't see what she's doing.

Pretend I'm not way too invested in making sure she's okay.

"What's all this?"

"My patient died."

"I'd pieced together that much. What happened?"

"Ah… Aneurysm, we think," she says, her attention fixed on some distant point over my shoulder that I can't reach.

"Did you do everything you could do?"

"Yeah." She swallows hard, and there's that chin tremble I knew was in there somewhere. "I did."

I believe her. She's cool-headed in emergencies and meticulous with her patients from everything I've seen. She's just starting out, but yeah. I believe her.

"Then let it go. Wall it off. Put it in a box. Move on."

Her attention zooms back to my face with a new intensity. I can almost feel her drawing the red bead in the dead center of my forehead.

"Like you do, you mean," she says sharply.

I hesitate. There's a trap here somewhere. I sense it even if I can't see it.

"Yeah. Like I do."

"Great." *Her eyes glitter as she flashes a chilling smile, the kind designed to strike you dead on the spot.* "I'll try to be more like you. Thanks for that life-changing advice, Dr. Jamison. If there's nothing else?"

Without waiting for me to answer, she wheels around and bangs into the nearest supply closet, her back ramrod straight.

I watch her go feeling hamstrung and impotent, fuming because I know there's something here that I don't get and because she makes me feel like my skin is way too tight.

Instead of letting it go and finding my patient, I barge into the supply closet after her.

"What's the issue, Harlow?" I demand gruffly, looking around to see where she's gone.

And discover her leaning against the wall with her hands over her face.

Sobbing.

My heart contracts hard enough for me to need one of the nearby crash carts. I don't know what I'm feeling here—I'm afraid to diagnose it—but I know it hurts.

"It's nothing," she says, now hurriedly wiping her eyes with the back of her hand. "I just need a minute."

"Don't lie to me."

I'm sure she puts my sudden harshness down to me being an inveterate asshole. Which is ideal. As long as she never knows that I can't take the sight of her tears. Not like this. If she needs me to kill someone for her, I will. Resurrect someone. Find someone. Buy something. Build something. Anything she needs, I'm here.

Anything to stop her from hurting like this.

And maybe there's a part of me that's spoiling for a fight because my world has been off-kilter since she showed up and I can't figure out how to set it straight again.

"My patient was a thirty-four-year-old man whose new fiancée brought him in because he had an episode of vertigo while they were cooking dinner." Ally's face is red and contorted. Her voice sounds thick and shaky. "Spaghetti with sausage. His name was Saul. I was asking him whether he also felt nausea when he grabbed his head and started screaming. Screaming. It was downhill from there. He crashed. I paged Dr. Smith. Who did everything he could."

I watch her, stricken. Fascinated.

"Saul died. I'm a medical professional and I'm still trying to figure out how someone could be alive and excited about getting married one minute and dead ten minutes later," she says, pausing to press her lips together. I get the feeling she's trying to hold back more sobs, and I can't blame her. "I can't begin to imagine how his fiancée feels, Lauren. So I am upset, Dr. Jamison. Unlike you, I am a human being. I have feelings."

"What?"

"Maybe you've heard of them? I can't always put them in a box and pretend they're not there. We can't all be a sphinx all the time. Sometimes those pesky feelings leak out. You caught me at a low moment. Obviously. I'm not up for being a robot right now. But don't worry. I'll try to be like you again tomorrow."

The outrageous injustice of this accusation threatens to choke me out. Utter paralysis shuts me down while I try to get my jaw unstuck enough to defend myself. But the effort gets delayed while I clench and unclench my fists and remind myself that it probably wouldn't be a good idea to give in to my frustration and rampage through this closet knocking everything off the shelves.

My only consolation? That she clearly has no idea how attracted I am to her and how it takes years of my life pretending I'm not.

Hopefully, I can keep it that way.

"Let me assure you, Dr. Harlow, that you don't know one fucking thing about me or my feelings and how I manage them," I say, my gruff voice deathly quiet as I stare her dead in the face and try not to get lost in those teary brown eyes. "Never presume that you do."

With all these heightened emotions flying around, I've forgotten myself and edged a little too close to her. Into the danger zone. For one arrested moment, I stare down at her and she stares up at me. At this range, it's easy to see the dewiness of her lips. The rosy perfection of her skin. The streaks of blond and the wisps of hair on either side of her amazing face. The striations of white, black and gold in her irises. During these suspended seconds, when my heart pounds in my throat, I fervently wish I *could fuck her up against that wall right there. Almost as much as I hope to never lay eyes on her again.*

Some of this must show in my face despite all my best efforts to keep it hidden. Her breath hitches. Her eyes widen. Her attention dips, just for a second, to my mouth.

And the reins of my control slip almost all the way out of my hands.

"Dr. Jamison," she says, her voice breathy.

I hear it in her tone.

The desire. The need.

They perfectly mirror what's going on inside me.

I want to be a good guy who can look himself in the mirror. But right now? I'm telling you, it could go either way. And I'm seriously starting to wonder what point there is to being an honorable human being when you're this fucking miserable.

But…

By some miracle, I manage to back up a step and turn away from her.

"Stop crying, Harlow. Pull your shit together." I sweep the door open for her. "Get back to work."

She blinks then hurries stiffly through the door without looking at me.

And promptly gets plowed down from the side by someone rushing by with a supply cart whose shouted warning comes too late.

Ally goes flying. I won't attempt to describe her yelp of pain or the sound of her precious skull intersecting with the hard linoleum floor. I don't need to get into how red her blood is against the golden hair. Her sudden absolute stillness as she lies there, facedown and unconscious, is forever seared into my brain. Never in my life, before or since, have I felt that sort of cataclysmic terror.

It was her injury, yeah, but I feel like these are also my scars.

"Hey! Moron!" Furious honking jars me out of my thoughts. I look around and discover that I'm on my way out of the park and crossing against the light. Some asshole leans his head out of his black Mercedes sedan so he can glare at me while giving me the one-fingered salute. "People are driving here! You want to get killed? Jump off the Brooklyn Bridge and leave the rest of us out of it!"

Backing up, I wave him through the intersection and try to regulate my breath as I cool down and head back to my office. The sun is lower in the sky now. I'm drenched with sweat. Guess I had a good jog. I'll never know. I feel like a sleepwalker who wakes up in a dark kitchen and discovers he's in the middle of making a peanut butter sandwich. No idea how I got here.

My thoughts go straight back to Ally and me dropping to the floor beside her as I shout for a neck brace and a backboard. Her physical exam. Her scans. Her concussion, which was severe enough to land her in the hospital for the night.

My vigil.

I let myself into her room later that night, when the floor is dark and quiet and I know she's likely to be asleep. Sure enough, she's resting comfortably with all that hair fanned out across her pillow. A modern-day sleeping beauty that's a million times more beautiful than anything Disney could produce.

I stand by her bed. Study her.

She's got long lashes. Really long. Her breathing is quiet and even. The bandage against her hairline is the one that I put there after I closed her laceration. I should've let a resident do it, but I wasn't about to trust anyone else with the job. Not with Ally.

I should go home. I know I should.

But I pull up the lounge chair, sink into it and stare at Ally while the realization sinks in.

I'm really fucked here.

I've been married for one year. My wife and I may be discovering that we don't know—or maybe like—each other as well as we thought we did, but that's marriage. Right? You hit rough patches. You get through them. I don't have the right to be this attracted to someone else. What am I going to do? Have an affair? Torpedo my marriage? My wife doesn't deserve that. Ally doesn't deserve to be ensnared in my mess. They both deserve so much better.

I'm not a horny college kid. I know there are consequences to my actions. I can keep it in my pants. Attractions come. Attractions go. The world keeps spinning.

But...

The thing is...

There's nothing like seeing someone injured—maybe even dead, for all you know—to make you realize that maybe there's more than an attraction going on there. Which means that things are a hell of a lot more complicated than you feared.

What the fuck am I supposed to do now? I really wish someone would tell me.

She sighs just then, an intimate, domestic sound that tugs on something primal deep inside me. I'm not supposed to hear sounds like that. Not from Ally. Just like I'll never see her in bed again after this. I'll certainly never touch her in bed. Which is as it should be.

It drives me crazy that I can't decide whether I like Ally as much as I think I do or whether my infatuation with her is a convenient way for me to keep one foot out the door of my marriage. But it seems like either option is a pretty bad sign for my relationship with my wife.

I'm good at handling medical emergencies. What I can't deal

with is this emotional purgatory of being profoundly glad that she's okay and simultaneously wrecked that she'll never be mine.

I rest my elbows on my knees, press the heels of my hands into my eyes and give in to the despair for a second. A sob without sobbing. A scream without screaming.

Then I pull my shit together like I told her to do earlier and raise my head, slump back in the lounge chair and remind myself that I belong at home. With my wife. And I'll go. In a little while. As soon as I satisfy myself that Ally's truly okay.

My movements make the chair squeak just then. Ally sighs again before turning her head in my direction and drowsily opening her eyes.

We lock gazes before her lids drift closed again. She starts to smile and reaches for my hand. Without hesitation. I scoot forward in my chair and take her hand. Without hesitation.

Her hand is soft. Her grip is strong. Her skin is vibrant.

"I'm not crazy," she murmurs as she rolls to her side, facing me while keeping firm possession of my hand. "I knew you'd be here."

I feel a surge of something powerful in my heart's frantic beat.

Joy. Relief. Acknowledgment.

I feel it. She feels it. Neither one of us is imagining things.

Her breathing evens out again, and I give myself thirty seconds to wallow in this interlude. I lace and unlace our fingers. I slide my palm across hers. I trace the pink ovals of her fingernails. I imagine what it would be like to be in bed with Ally at the end of a long shift at the hospital, watching TV or discussing our individual days. I press a fervent and lingering kiss to the back of her hand.

Then I let her go, make sure she's nicely tucked in, go home to my wife and put my back into my efforts to be a good husband.

That night, I make a pledge to myself. The universe or God

or whoever has done the right thing and kept Ally safe. I should also do the right thing. I can't be a half-assed husband. I can't be a snake who gives Ally mixed signals.

So I won't.

That's why I avoid Ally a couple of days later when she returns to work. And that's how I generate the performance of my lifetime when, late in the shift, she materializes at my side while I'm typing up a patient note.

"Dr. Jamison," she says, a false note of cheer in her voice. "I'm back."

Please. Like I didn't feel a disturbance in the Force the second she walked through the sliding glass doors into the building this morning.

"Oh, yeah?" I say, still typing. "Headache? Nausea? Dizziness? Confusion?"

I think I detect a frown, but I can't be sure because I'm determined not to look directly at her.

"A slight, ah, headache, but that's all," she says.

"Good. You haven't screwed up my handiwork, have you?"

"Not so far," she says, touching her bandage.

She sounds wounded now.

And there's only so much acting I can do. I'm not Leonardo fucking DiCaprio.

"Great." I finish typing, grab my coffee and turn to go, determined to get away from her as soon as possible. Before my fragile resolve collapses entirely. "Back to work, then."

I make it one step away. Two steps. On the third step, I start to congratulate myself on a clean getaway, but then I hear her voice behind me.

"You didn't…"

Shit. Fuck.

I stiffen and turn back, trying to look annoyed.

"Didn't what, Harlow?" I say, checking my watch to avoid looking her in the eye. "I've got surgery."

She tries to smile like it's nothing, but I know exactly what she's about to ask.

Trust me. It's not nothing.

"You didn't stop by my room to check on me the other night, did you?"

I look directly at her. The vulnerable hope in her expression kills me.

Kills. Me.

But I stick the landing.

"No. Why would I?" I say, trying to look politely puzzled by the idea. I watch the hurt creep into her expression, quickly followed by unmistakable bewilderment as she looks away, her face shadowed. No doubt she's replaying the whole episode in her mind and trying to decide if she's crazy or not. I hate myself for gaslighting her. But not as much as I'd hate myself for fucking up three lives by following my attraction to her to its natural conclusion and cheating on my wife. "I knew you were in good hands. We done?"

To her immense credit, she blinks and gets all her shields in place. If I'm lucky, she'll decide she imagined or dreamed the whole thing as a side effect of her concussion. If I'm not lucky, she'll put me down as a spineless and lying MF'er.

Either way, she'll stay away from me. The way I'm determined to stay away from her for the duration of her internship.

"We're done," she says crisply, taking off and leaving me to stare after her.

But we weren't done. Not then, and not now.

But I am done with my shower. I can only hide out in the stall for so long, and it's unrealistic for me to expect a little soap and water to dissipate all the tension buzzing through my body.

Sighing, I kill the water and get out. I'm toweling off my head when another memory of Ally hits me. I've got a million of them. Ally the night of the dinner cruise, with that sexy dress and the breeze ruffling her hair. Her eyes. Her smile. Her *mouth*. A shiver runs across my cooling skin, igniting nerve endings far and wide. From there, it doesn't take much to get my dick fired up. And there it is. More tension.

Wonderful.

"Thanks, Harlow." I eyeball the haggard and hollow-eyed loser in the mirror with absolute disgust as I sling the towel around my shoulders and grip myself. This is what I've come to. Lusting after my employee. Who, by the way, is some other guy's girlfriend. Jacking off to a playlist of her images in the bathroom at work. *"Pathetic."*

Without warning, the door swings open.

And that's how Ally finds me. With only a towel and a pair of flip-flops keeping me from being butt-ass naked. Pumping my rock-hard dick like my life depends on it.

Our gazes connect in the mirror.

I freeze.

She freezes.

Actually, her lower jaw hits the floor. *Then* she freezes.

An awkward eternity passes, completing my humiliation.

"I just needed to use…" She trails off, her face flooding with vivid color as she gives me a swift once-over that encompasses everything. If I've got a zit on my left butt cheek, I'm guessing she sees it. "The, ah, bathroom."

"It's not exactly a good time." I hastily snatch the towel from my neck, sling it around my hips and secure it. The best I can do, but not the ideal disguise for a throbbing and insistent erection that seems determined to reach her from all the way across the room. "Go somewhere else."

"I didn't think anyone was here," she continues, flustered. "Why didn't you lock the—"

"*Harlow*. Get. The. Fuck. Out."

My booming voice galvanizes her. Thank God.

"Sorry," she cries, backing out and slamming the door behind her.

Leaving me to call myself every name in the book and wonder how the hell I think I'm ever going to look her in the eye again.

10

"I NEED YOU. Where the hell are you?" I ask Kelly a little while later when I video-call her from the packed bar. After grabbing my forgotten phone from my desk drawer and *trying* to use the bathroom at the office, I checked on a couple more patients before heading straight here. I found an empty table by some miracle. Now I'm starting on my second margarita, grateful that she and I had the foresight to schedule another girls' night ahead of time. It's not like her to be late, and my frazzled nerves can't tolerate anything else going side-ways on me tonight. Then I get a closer look at her. "Hang on. What's with the mask?"

"I'm obviously minimizing my pores," she says, gingerly touching the edge of the white tissue mask covering her face. She's also wearing a fluffy spa robe and hair towel, I realize. My heart sinks. Meeting me for drinks is clearly the last thing on her mind. "What's the problem?"

"We're supposed to be having girls' night," I say,

rising impatience and frustration making me shrill. "How could you blow me off like this?"

"I'm not blowing you off, dingbat. It's tomorrow."

"It is not tomorrow." My looming personal crisis does not prevent me from quickly scrolling through our texts so I can prove her wrong and gloat. I never make airheaded mistakes like this. "It says right here that we're meeting...*tomorrow* night. Oh my God."

Deflated, I put the phone down and slump over the table with my head in my hands.

"Did someone die?" she says, sounding bemused. "I can de-mask and get over there, but it'll take a while."

"It's fine." I straighten again and glumly reach for my margarita. "I'll survive."

"What happened? Don't keep me in suspense." The mask ruins the effect of the stern look she tries to give me, but I get what she's going for. "And I'm telling you right now—if it has anything to do with the Sphinx, prepare for me to reach through the phone and kick your butt."

My morale plummets even further. The situation is truly dire if I'm desperate enough to submit to another lecture about the evils of my sexy boss.

"It's not that big a deal. It's just that I saw him naked a little while ago. He was coming out of the shower at the office." I decide to leave out the part about him jacking off. No need to share *all* the gory details. "Now my brain is poisoned by the image."

"Oh my God," she cries, appropriately scandalized. "Why wouldn't he lock the door?"

"I know! That's what I said! No idea. I guess he forgot."

"And...?"

I open my mouth and try to throw together a sentence or two to describe him, but the English language only has two hundred thousand words or so. It's just not equipped to do justice to a man like Dr. Jamison.

Let's just say that I couldn't believe it when I walked into the bathroom and saw him in all his glory. I feel like I double-dipped because I came up behind him but was still able to see his front in the mirror. What can I say? I'm a lucky girl. I've never swooned before in my life, but I came close at the sight of him. The toned calves. The powerful thighs. The round ass. I'm not an ass-biter under normal conditions, but I'd absolutely make an exception for him. He's got narrow hips. Chiseled chest and shoulders. Ladder-rung abs with zero discernible fat. All that tawny skin. The dusting of black hair across his pecs and the way it narrows to parts below before flaring out again. The strong column of his throat as he leaned his head back. His parted lips. His eyes, heavy-lidded with passion and glimmering a vivid blue in the light.

The parts below…

No words.

Strike that. I *do* have words:

Thick. Long. Ruddy.

Tempting.

Let's just say that the good Dr. Jamison gave himself a true and unforgettable handful.

Oh, the things a dick like that could do for a woman lucky enough to find out. I can only imagine the exquisite pleasure. And what was he thinking about at that moment that made it so hard? Was he watching porn on his phone or something? Thinking about the gorgeous woman he's no doubt hooking up with later?

Someone tall and thin who's probably never struggled with her weight and enjoys drinking bone broth for dinner every night?

What I wouldn't give for a night in bed with Dr. Jamison, his flashing blue eyes and that body. There. I said it. I know I'm in a committed relationship with whatshisname. *Bruce.* I know I'm not supposed to think about another man's body sliding into place between my thighs.

But what am I supposed to do here? How can I unsee what I already saw?

Beholding Dr. Jamison like that provoked a fierce and primal response from my body. My nose still remembers his freshly showered scent and seems to have blocked all other smells from my nostrils. My heart rate hasn't returned to normal, and at this point I wonder if it ever will. My face feels flushed. My lips and nipples still tingle. All the tiny hidden muscles between my thighs keep clenching and unclenching, needing relief. I'm convinced that if I spent another thirty seconds in that steamy bathroom with him, I'd have emerged pregnant with triplets.

"Ally? How did he look?" Kelly asks. I swear she's holding her breath.

"How do you think?" I ask bitterly, then reach for my margarita and down the rest of it in two big gulps.

"Damn," she mutters. "I was hoping he had a tiny dick or something."

"No such luck."

"Well, I'm sorry you had to see that, Ally," she says. "But you can't let it get inside your head. You just need to, I don't know, block it out."

"Block it out? Are you insane? Would *you* be able to block it out?"

"Look. I leave it to you, your conscience and your vibrator. What the three of you do on your own time is your business. I'm just saying that you've got something good going with Bruce. *Please* don't let the Sphinx back into your head again. He's not good for you. You know he's not."

"I know, I know," I say, reminding myself of the way he blew up at me today. Twice. Here I am tied up in knots over him and he can't, even now, treat me with basic respect. He still barks at me as though I'm his lowly intern. And I'm so stupid that I take the barking and somehow twist it into…

I don't even know what to call it.

He agitates and aggravates me. He works his way into my brain like a mole digging his tunnel. He turns my own hormones against me. He scrambles all my circuits and puts my thoughts into a blender. And when he turns the blender off, lifts the lid and pours out the contents, what emerges is complete nonsense. I imagine that he's looking at me a certain kind of way. That there's a funny note in his voice. That there's a hidden meaning in what he says. That he stands too close or lingers too long.

God, he's turning me into a freaking Bonnie Raitt song.

Spending time with him makes me foolish. Pathetic. I may as well be the awkward high school freshman lusting after the homecoming king. Do you think the homecoming king ever notices the freshman trailing him around like a clingy golden retriever puppy? No. Of course not. That only ever happens in Molly Ringwald movies from the eighties.

How I think I'm going to work successfully with him this year is anyone's guess. But I'm getting sick of myself and this self-destructive weakness I have for him.

I'm getting *really* sick of it.

"You know what? I'm fine," I tell Kelly, taking a deep breath and trying my best to mean it. "I'm not letting that man get inside my head like this. He's sexy. I knew that already. This is not new information. And you know what? I have the perfect antidote to his sexiness. You know what it is? He's a jackass. He treats me like a peon. I just need to remember that the next time I start thinking about his perfect body."

"Good for you. That's all you can do, right?" She produces a glass of red wine and toasts me with it. "Fight the darkness."

"Exactly. And Bruce is coming this weekend so we can check out apartments."

"Focus on your future with Bruce. Hopefully the two of you will find a fantastic apartment that's rent-controlled—"

"Hang on," I say, diverted by the departure of the group sitting at the table directly in front of me. Now that they're gone, I catch a glimpse of a guy sitting alone at a small booth against the far wall. A guy with dark hair and stern features on his downturned face. A guy who swirls the amber drink in his tumbler and looks as though he'd like to drown himself in it. "Oh my God. It's him."

"Who?"

"Dr. Jamison," I say, my blood pressure skyrocketing.

As though he feels the sudden weight of my attention, he looks up, sees me seeing him, scowls, kills most of his drink and signals to the server for a refill.

"He just scowled at me," I tell Kelly, outrage getting the best of me. "So let's make that *three* times today he's been a jerk to me."

"*Bastard*," she says with the fervency I require from her as my best friend.

"You know what? I'm hanging up. I'm going to go talk to him." I've had just enough alcohol for this to seem like a good idea. "Stand up for myself for once. Tell him I'm sick of this routine."

"I don't know about that," she says, looking worried. "I don't want you saying something to get yourself fired from your great new job. I know how you are when you get mad."

"That's a price I'll just have to pay." I abruptly stand, making my chair scrape and drawing his attention again. He hits me with an additional scowl, which only fuels my fierce desire to borrow someone's drink and dump it in his lap. "Wish me luck."

"Don't do anything stupid," she says. "Call me later and let me know how it went."

"Will do."

I hang up, grab my purse and weave my way over to his booth. He watches me the whole way, his lowered brows a whole mood by themselves as he finishes off his drink and sets the glass down. There's an indecipherable gleam of something new in his eyes tonight—something that seems vaguely dangerous—but I suppose that's what being caught masturbating will do for a person.

"Dr. Jamison," I say stiffly.

His jaw tightens as he slings an arm across the top of his seat and looks up at me. "Harlow."

"Mind if I join you? We need to talk."

"Not tonight."

I hesitate. Having worked up the indignation to come over here, I didn't expect him to refuse. The server arrives with his refill just then, knocking me further off-kilter. But, on the other hand, the distraction gives me a second to shore up my courage. I'm not going anywhere. The two of us need to come to a new understanding.

"Thanks," he tells the server, who walks off. "Anything else, Harlow?"

"Yes," I say, hiking up my chin as I slide into the booth opposite him. My heart is about to skitter into cardiac arrest, but he doesn't need to know that. "I want to talk about the way you treat me."

Those heavy brows creep up. "The way I…?"

"Treat me, yes," I say. "I'm sick of it."

A humorless smile flickers by, leaving an imprint on his face. "You don't want to engage me tonight, Harlow." His tone is calm. Flat. It's also intensely disquieting. "Trust me. Go home. Call your boyfriend. We'll pretend we never saw each other."

"No," I say, my overwhelming nerves making me shaky now. "You don't get to set the agenda."

There's an excruciating pause while he cocks his head and squints at me as though he wants to make sure he hasn't lapsed into a hallucination.

"I don't get to set the agenda?"

"You *bark* at me. You *scowl* at me. You order me around like I'm still your lowly little intern—"

"Oh, I do?" He abruptly changes positions, putting his elbows down and leaning in to hunker over the table. He's much closer now, and the relentless intensity in those glittering eyes is deeply unsettling. No wonder they call him the Sphinx. I can't decide whether he's trying to intimidate me or laughing at me. Either option activates my defiant streak. "What else? This is fascinating."

"I'll tell you what else. If you think I'm going to work with you treating me like —"

"You *will* work with me. We have a contract. Unless you want me to sue you into oblivion."

"Don't you dare threaten me," I say, mirroring his posture and leaning in. "I'm not trying to get out of my contract. That's not even what this is about."

"Then what *is* it about, pray?"

"I want you to stop taking your shitty moods out on me."

"Why? You cause them."

"What?" I'm so stung by the injustice of this accusation that the word erupts out of me. "I've never done anything to you!"

"That's the fucking stupidest thing you've ever said, Harlow," he says without missing a beat. He looks murderous now. "You should be smart enough to notice when a guy loses his head over you. Especially when it's been going on for four years."

"I'm a complete professional and a team player — Wait, *what*?"

Sudden catastrophic shock shuts me completely down while we stare at each other and the rest of the world drops away. Between my pounding heart and my heaving lungs, I absolutely cannot catch my breath. All I can do is sit there, gaping and mute.

Waiting.

He blinks, looking as surprised that he said it as I am to hear it. He presses his lips together hard enough to make a muscle clench in his jaw. I get the feeling he wants to take it back. But he surprises me. Again.

"You know I want you, Harlow," he says, his voice hoarse.

I manage a shaky breath. "I don't know anything. Maybe you should tell me."

He hesitates in the pregnant silence.

Then something abruptly shifts in his expression, lighting up his entire face.

"I think about you," he says. "The things you say. The way you laugh. Your smile. Your *eyes*."

I shake my head because I cannot be hearing these things from him. I cannot be seeing this urgency. In *him*. As though the words have been stockpiled and hidden inside him this whole time and he can't manage the burden of repressing them for another second.

"I've been trying to be a good guy. This whole time," he continues. "I need to be able to look myself in the mirror. My marriage vows meant something. If you're in a committed relationship with Bruce, that means something. I want to respect that." He shrugs, looking stricken now. "But I can't do it. I can't keep quiet anymore. It's killing me, Harlow. It's *killing* me."

I'm still shaking my head. This scene is so surreal that that's all I'm able to manage for the longest time.

"This doesn't make sense to me," I finally tell him. My entire body feels as though it's trembling, down to the last strand of hair on my head. My shaky voice can barely manage the words. "I don't know what you're saying."

"I'm saying that for four years I have wondered about you."

"Wondered *what*?"

This seems to be the magic question. He can't get the words out fast enough. He seems *happy* to tell me.

"*Everything*. What you were like as a kid. Whether you have any pets. Where you like to go on vacation. What you read. What it's like to wake up with you in the morning. What it's like to watch TV with you."

I can't breathe. "Oh my God."

"There's more," he says, a sensual note creeping into his voice.

"I can't take any more."

"Too bad." His heated gaze dips lower, touching my mouth and lingering on the hint of cleavage beneath my T-shirt before slowly traveling back to my eyes. "I wonder what you taste like. *Everywhere*. I wonder what your pussy smells like. How hot and wet I can get you. I wonder how you like to be fucked. Anything you want would be my pleasure, but I'm old school. Missionary is my favorite. I want to see your face when you come for me. I want to *hear* you."

Images spring to life inside my overheated brain. Seething images. Illicit images.

They make my breath hitch audibly. I won't bore you with all the details about how they affect my nipples and pussy. Let's just say that it's profound.

"If you want to know what I was thinking about when you walked in on me jacking myself off this afternoon, it was *you*. It's always *you*."

I gape at him.

He shrugs.

The moment stretches into infinity.

"So." He sips his drink. Clears his throat. "Now you know."

The confession requires some response, but I can't seem to generate one. I'm too overwhelmed. Way too aroused.

"I don't know what to say," I finally tell him. "I don't know what to do here."

There's another pause, longer this time. "You could always threaten to sue me for sexual harassment," he says with a crooked smile.

As if. "I don't plan to do that."

"Good to know. *Say something.*"

If only I could. But all the turbulent feelings inside me make that impossible.

Shock. Disbelief. Relief mixed with triumph because I'm not crazy after all.

Maybe even creeping euphoria.

But…

How is this possible?

I can't believe that a man like *this* would ever think about me like *that*. I can't reconcile this sudden, unexpected intensity with the cool-eyed Dr. Jamison I've known this whole time. Nor can I sync it up with me and my extra twenty pounds and the things I know to be true about myself.

I'm not this special. Never have been, never could be.

I open my mouth, determined to talk some sense into him, to keep my head on straight and not get caught up in a fever dream where the two of us could somehow be together.

"You've acted like you didn't want me," I say. "This whole time."

"I know."

"Now I can't believe that you do," I say, unable to keep the wounded note out of my voice.

A wave of comprehension washes over his expression. "Ally. Look at me."

I don't know what's more damaging to my equilibrium: the tenderness and intimacy in his voice as he uses my first name for what I'm positive is only the second time ever, or the focused intensity with which he stares at me across the table.

He doesn't say anything and doesn't need to. It's all right there.

I think about all the times I wondered what was going on behind those cool eyes and wished I could find out. What secrets he might be keeping. This moment out of time is the perfect antidote to wipe all that away. The perfect reversal of everything that's happened before, the same way a dose of naloxone reverses a heroin overdose and wipes it clean.

I see it all in those few arrested seconds.

Desire. Need. Aching vulnerability that exactly matches what I'm feeling inside.

Even so, this is all too much to process over drinks at a bar. I don't know what I'm supposed to do here. Am I supposed to scuttle my entire relationship with Bruce just because this man finally crooked his little finger at me?

"I have a life, Dr. Jamison," I say, surging adrenaline making me shrill and fidgety. A booth this size can't contain the amount of energy coursing through my body. "Am I just supposed to drop to my knees in gratitude?"

"We should probably switch to first names at this point, Ally." The dry tone doesn't help.

"I had *plans*," I say.

"I know," he says quietly.

"They didn't include you."

He bows his head. "I'm sorry."

He seems to mean it, but that's not good enough.

Those two words don't get you off the hook when you've just lobbed a grenade into the middle of someone's life.

"You should be. Why should I drop everything for you? You didn't drop everything for *me*, did you? Matter of fact, you made me feel like I was crazy for thinking you were attracted to me. And now you snap your fingers and I'm supposed to come running?"

Everything closes off. It's like the Great Wall of China opening between us.

"Not at all," he says, but his calm demeanor doesn't quite match up with his banked turbulence as he stands, pulls out his wallet and tosses some money on the table. "If you want me, you know where to find me. Otherwise? Go call your boyfriend. Forget I ever said anything."

Forget?

I watch him, feeling strangely deflated as I repress the wild urge to ask if he's insane.

"But…"

"Up to you," he says with a final pointed glance at me. *"Harlow."*

I don't like this renewed use of my last name after the intimacy of the last several minutes. I don't like it at all.

I put my elbows on the table again and drop my head into my hands as he strides off, trapped in the aftershocks of this erupting emotional volcano and somehow resisting the urge to hurry after him.

The rest of the world simultaneously returns in a rush, bringing the renewed sound of the crowd's dull roar. My heart thumps. My hands tremble. A hysterical burble of laughter lingers in my throat.

And I absolutely cannot corral my racing thoughts.

I'm so shaken and frazzled that I snatch up my phone

when it buzzes and answer it without checking the display or bothering to keep the strain out of my voice. A costly rookie mistake.

"Dr. Harlow," I say.

"It's me, babe. Where are you? What's wrong?"

Oh, God. It's Bruce. Causing me to feel a fun new emotion: guilt.

Fuuuuck.

"Hey." I clear my throat, grateful this isn't a video call and determined to try again because my voice still sounds way too high and false. I also remind myself that I haven't done anything wrong. Sitting and listening while someone confesses to having feelings for me does not make me a villain. "I'm fine. I just, ah, stopped to get a drink before I went home. I got the nights mixed up with Kelly. It's supposed to be tomorrow."

"Is that why you're upset?"

I absolutely cannot deal with his concern right now. It makes me feel like a snake. Nor am I ready to have any sort of coherent conversation. Not with my thoughts churning like this.

"It's just a, ah, long day. I'll be fine. It's nothing."

Long silence from Bruce. "Why do I get the feeling you're lying to me?"

His bewilderment comes through loud and clear. So does his hurt.

That's when it hits me in a moment of terrifying clarity. He's absolutely right. What just happened isn't *nothing*, no matter how much I might wish it was. But I can't un-hear what Dr. Jamison told me. I can't un-feel my reaction to it.

What just happened is *everything* to me. Absolutely

life-changing. Meaning that I've allowed this developing situation to turn me into a liar.

Lying to an innocent party like Bruce is bad enough, but the truth is that I'm mostly lying to myself. What I just learned from Dr. Jamison—from *Michael*—means that things are over between me and Bruce. Even if I'm not quite ready to admit it aloud.

"Ally?"

"You're right," I admit quietly. "Let's talk about it this weekend. When you're here."

Stunned silence from Bruce.

Meanwhile, I press my lips together and furiously blink back a hot tear or two, determined to get through this conversation with grace and without crying. If I need to let Bruce go—which I do—the least I can do is behave like a grown woman about it and tell him to his face. That's the least he deserves.

"Fuck," he says, the syllable drenched in disbelief. "You're dumping me. Aren't you?"

My heart sinks and bottoms out somewhere near Tibet. This is obviously not a conversation I want to have while on the phone in the middle of a bar. "Bruce…"

"Just say it," he says, his tone turning harsh. "Don't leave me hanging for the next two days."

I take a deep breath. On the one hand, it's hard to hurt someone you care about. Hard to grab those over-sized emotional shears and cut someone out of your life. On the other hand, it's not hard at all. Not when I remember that the purpose of this conversation is to free me up to be with Michael.

That's what makes this whole situation so sad.

It's not that I never cared about Bruce, because I did. He's a great guy. We had fun together even if he never set my heart on fire. None of that was a lie. It's just that it's humbling to realize that I talked and fooled myself into believing that I could be indifferent to Michael's reappearance in my life when I *knew*, on a cellular level, that all he ever had to do was say the word and I'd be there. That maybe I was only ever biding my time with Bruce, hoping that a star or two would align and bring Michael across my path again. Married or not, I can't honestly say that I'd care. Maybe that makes me a bigger fool than I ever suspected.

I just know that it's Michael. It's always been *Michael*.

If I'd been honest with myself all along, I'd never have entertained the idea of Bruce moving to NYC to be with me. Now Bruce will suffer because of my self-denial. And I know, in my heart of hearts, that once I'm with Michael, I'll never give Bruce a second thought.

Does that make me a horrible person? A selfish person?

Maybe. And the stain on my conscience of knowing that I hurt someone because of my carelessness is something I'll have to live with.

But I can't sugarcoat things with Bruce and pretend that the two of us have a chance when I know that we don't. That'll only make things worse for him in the long run.

"I don't think things are going to work out between us, yes," I say.

"There's someone else, isn't there? That's why you've been so distant. Don't deny it."

Oh, how I wish I hadn't just put on my big-girl panties. I really want to deny it. Taking the coward's way out seems like a mighty seductive option right now. It sure would make my life easier. But I don't want to be a coward on top of everything else.

"Nothing's happened, but…yes."

"Hang on," he says, and I can almost hear the whirring as his brain puts two and two together and easily comes up with four. "It's your boss, isn't it?"

"Yes," I reluctantly admit.

"Wait a minute. Wait one fucking minute. It was *him*, wasn't it? The guy you said you were into back during your internship? It was your boss, wasn't it?"

I cringe, wishing I'd never confided about my battle with depression and the reasons behind it to him. "Bruce…"

"Wasn't it?"

"Yes."

"And you agreed to work for this guy? Right under my nose while I'm living in some other city trying to figure out a way to be with you? Is *that* what I deserve?"

What can I say? He's absolutely right. And I'm ashamed of myself.

"I'm so sorry—"

"Save it. Good fucking riddance."

"Bruce," I say, but the line is already dead.

I lower the phone and stare at it in my hand, hating myself for the soaring relief I feel now that that difficult conversation is over.

11

MICHAEL

WELL, you really screwed that up, champ, my brain jeers at me as I step out of my private elevator into my apartment, click on the lights and toss my keys and wallet onto the foyer console a little while later.

Screwed. That. Up.

How? Let me count the ways.

First off, masturbating in an unlocked bathroom *at work*? Not a good look.

Second, drinking while upset is never a good idea. So there's that.

Third, and this is a biggie, I abandoned my moral compass and became exactly the kind of snake I'd hoped never to be. So much for being a good guy and respecting someone else's relationship. So much for doing the right thing. Yeah, I tried as best I could, but so what? I don't give myself half credit for trying any more than I'd pat myself on the back for feeding the poor if I ate their dinner on the way to the shelter to serve it to them.

Fourth, spewing feelings while buzzed is also the

height of foolishness. Every idiotic college freshman who's survived his or her first semester has already learned that lesson the hard way. So congrats on being stupider than the average eighteen-year-old, asshole. I didn't formulate a plan for telling Ally how I feel. Didn't strategize proposals or next steps. I just opened my mouth and vomited it all up like said idiot college freshman regurgitating shots. As a man who prides himself on his wisdom and tact (*I'm* the guy that my sister and all my friends turn to when they need a level head and some common sense, for fuck's sake), I'm shaken and vaguely terrified to discover that I've reached this low point where I have so little control over myself where she's concerned.

Finally and most horrifying? Having made the questionable decision to tell her the truth, I did it in the worst possible way. I didn't woo her. There was no romance. No finesse. Just me at my gruff worst, barking out non sequiturs about thinking about her and wanting to fuck her.

I mean, seriously, dude? What's compelling about that? Where's the game in that? Where's the skill? Having finally worked up the courage (liquid though it was) to tell Ally how I feel, the very least I could have done would be to put a little sparkle on it. Let her know how truly special I think she is.

But no. I fucked it all the way up. I didn't just shoot myself in the foot, I pulled out a semiautomatic rifle and blew all my poor toes to smithereens. Then, to close it all out, I told her to go call her boyfriend rather than, say, pleading for her to give me a chance and promising to worship the ground she walks on if she does.

Of *course* she didn't react with unrestrained joy and

leap onto my lap in the middle of the bar. Of *course* she didn't promise to leave her nice-guy boyfriend for me after the performance I gave. Why would she?

I shake my head at myself and top it off with a bitter and disbelieving laugh.

Well done, Jamison. Truly exemplary.

At least the cat's out of the bag, I decide as I kick my shoes into the basket next to the elevator then get a little more comfortable by shedding my T-shirt and jeans and dumping them on the bench before tossing my phone onto the living room sofa and heading straight to the bar area. At least I don't have to pretend around her anymore. And you know what? It was a relief to tell her. I feel light and airy, as though I've wriggled my way out from under the two-ton boulder that's been flattening me this whole time. I can breathe again. Although that feeling will probably only last as long as it takes her to sue me for sexual harassment. I should probably call my lawyers and tell them to be on the lookout for her lawsuit. Maybe give them a little extra retainer.

I splash some scotch and soda into a crystal tumbler and stare at my glittering skyline view of the Hudson River in a moody silence. I've never felt like more of a loser, which is ironic, given the fact that I'm at the top of my game. I've made a fortune from my investment in Liam's medical device. I bought myself this fantastic penthouse apartment. Started furnishing it. I've got cars and clothes. I travel if I ever eke out any free time, which I don't particularly want to do, because I'm having so much fun building my new practice group. I have almost everything a person could want or need to live his best life.

Except the *one* woman I can't stop thinking about.

I sip my drink, but the taste sours in my mouth. I set the tumbler on the coffee table and slump onto the sofa with my hands on top of my head. Swear to God, I'm so frustrated, I could grab handfuls of my hair and rip it out by the roots. I'm still so hot for her that I could beat my meat again. Hopefully to completion this time. Except that the idea holds zero appeal. And I'm too emotionally exhausted to bother anyway.

So…

I guess that leaves TV. I could try to find a good murder documentary. Those always cheer me up. Maybe the background noise will distract me while I try to figure out how I'm going to face her at work tomorrow after all this.

I reach for the remote, but my phone buzzes before I can hit any buttons. I seriously consider letting it go to voicemail, since I'm not on call tonight and the effort to answer it requires way more energy than I currently possess. But then it buzzes again and I answer out of habit.

"Yeah?"

"Dr. Jamison, it's Frederick downstairs." Building security.

"Yep," I say, rubbing my eyes with my free hand. "What's up?"

"I have someone here to see you, but her name isn't on your approved list. Do you know an Ally?"

I frown, my brain blanking completely out for a good three or four seconds.

Then it hits me with the force of a lightning strike through the top of my head.

"Ally?" I say, shooting to my feet. "What the fuck are you doing, Freddie? Send her up. *Now.*"

"Right away, sir."

I toss the phone away and add another transgression to my list of sins for the night: acting like a jackass to the security guy. I'll give him a nice tip tomorrow.

For now, I race to my elevator, my heart in my throat and my clumsy limbs feeling as though they belong to some other guy. Nerves will do that to you. It's a wonder I don't trip over my own feet and make it the rest of the way sprawled on my belly like a batter sliding into home plate. Throwing my clothes back on never crosses my mind. It's all I can do to work my lungs in a semi-normal manner and try to manage the rest of this body that feels as though it's trembling with anticipation.

Then the doors slide open and there she is. Right out of my wildest dreams.

She seems as breathless as I feel. Her color is high. There's a thrilling and fiery light in her whiskey-colored eyes that I've never seen before, and that makes my blood sizzle with anticipation.

I wait, holding myself in ruthless check and not daring to move as she steps off the elevator. If she's here to tell me I'll be hearing from her lawyers, my plan is to go throw myself out of one of my overpriced windows and be done with the misery.

She tries to smile, gesturing helplessly.

"Why didn't you say so?"

My entire body sags with relief before threatening to explode with euphoria. I start to reach for her but catch myself. One crucial detail needs clarification before we go any further.

"I'm not sharing you. I'm not playing games. I've waited too long for this." I hesitate, mentally kicking myself for bringing up a topic that could scuttle the proceedings before they even get started. But I'm dead serious here. "What about Bruce?"

Those glorious eyes smile at me.

And I am *lost*.

"There's no Bruce," she says quietly. "There's just you."

That's all I need to hear.

I make a guttural sound of triumph and relief as I pull her into my arms, then almost need to push her away again. The shock of finally touching her is so great that it overloads all my systems.

"Fuck." I help myself to her hair, awed by the thickness of that fragrant silk. I press my nose to the warmth of her scalp, rooting for her scent. *Vanilla*. There it is. I hold her closer, reveling in the supple planes of her back. Her fierce strength as she tightens her arms around me and runs *her* fingers through *my* hair. She's as eager and desperate as I am, murmuring indistinct words of encouragement that drive me out of my freaking mind. I run my hands down to her juicy ass, all but coming on the spot as I thrust against her. My dick, so long denied where she's concerned, has no manners tonight. No patience. Sadly, there's nothing I can do about it, and no one should expect otherwise. Would you require me to take leisurely sips of water through a cocktail straw after crawling across the Sahara Desert? I don't think so.

But...

I do want to savor this moment. At least for a second.

So I palm her velvety cheeks between my hands, stare down at those luminous eyes and try to comprehend what's happening here. I'm not lying when I tell you I feel as though I'm touching an angel. A sultry angel who understands the effects she has on a man's body, mind you, but still an angel of whom I am not worthy and probably never will be. No matter how hard I try. My mouth works in absolute silence, overflowing with a huge backlog of things I want to tell her yet unable to find a single word.

Where would I start? How would I begin to tell her how beautiful she is and how good she feels? How grateful I am? How I swear—I *swear*—she'll never regret making the decision to be with me? I'm a scientist, not a poet. I'd need to deputize Shakespeare and get him in here to pinch-hit for me. But I doubt even he could do her justice.

In the end, I snap my jaws shut again and shake my head at myself. She'll just have to understand that that's all I can manage. The flash of her responsive smile tells me that we're on the exact same page here.

This is happening. It's real. We both know it. No further communication necessary.

Groaning helplessly, I duck my head and kiss those lush lips.

Something snaps inside my head, shocking me and forcing me to break the contact. I don't know what the hell it is because I've never felt it before. Probably the implosion of all those sizzling nerve endings, generating sparks. But it forces me to pause and try to catch my breath. Difficult to do when her wide eyes, glittering and heavy-lidded now, are the only things I can see. She's tremulous. *I'm* tremulous. I get the distinct feeling that I'm biting off a million times more than I can chew. Like a kid who thinks he knows how to ride a Harley just because he stole the keys and figured out how to peddle his big wheel down the driveway. I don't know where this is going between us.

There's only one thing I know for sure:

We are not. Fucking. Stopping. Now.

I kiss her again, my lips gliding over hers as I angle her head and go deeper. We urgently try different ways that our mouths can fit together, getting the feel of each other and exploring every possibility as I slowly back her toward the console. We nip, suck and lick. We whisper heated encouragement to each other. She drags her hands all over my bare back and shoulders. I don't neglect the gym, so hopefully she likes what she feels. I certainly like the feeling of her round ass in my hands and my dick thrusting against her soft pussy, I'll tell you that.

But she's wearing way more clothes than I am, and I *don't* like that. I've been dying to see these breasts. For *years*. I don't plan to wait another second longer than I need to.

I reach up and disentangle her greedy hands from around my neck, ignoring her incoherent sound of disapproval as I push her back just enough to open some space between us so I can figure out what to do to get her naked. She's wearing a sexy black sundress with skinny straps and a million buttons marching down the front. It takes me one second to decide I'm not dealing with that shit. There's no time.

Shooting her an apologetic look, I take the two halves of the dress right below her collarbones and yank them in opposite directions from top to bottom. This generates the supremely satisfying sounds of the dress ripping out of my way, all those buttons skittering across the floor and, best of all, her knowing laughter.

Glad she's not mad.

But any relief I feel to be closer to her vibrant skin is

short-lived once I catch sight of her strapless bra. Also black. That'll also have to go. I yank the thing down—who the hell knows whether the clasp is in the front or the back?—and am rewarded by the sight of her pale breasts bouncing back into place. My breath catches at this bounty. She's got bright pink nipples that are the exact shade of her lips. The nipples are pointy. Hard. Waiting. I bend and dive in with my hands and then my mouth, a distant corner of my fried brain wondering who's making the crazed animal sounds and deciding that it's probably me.

As a breast guy, I could probably pull up a chair and have myself a good old time right here. Especially with her arms locked in place around my head, holding me exactly where I want to be, and her unabashed coos of appreciation spurring me on. But the chances of me losing control and ejaculating all over her and my brand-new foyer like Prince's purple guitar at that Super Bowl several years back keep growing exponentially by the second. The last thing I want to do tonight is embarrass myself and let her down.

So, with regret, I let the current nipple pop out of my mouth and rip her panties—black lace; very nice—past the sexy expanse of her hips and down her thighs, out of my way. Obviously, I can't miss a chance to taste that pussy, so I don't. I give her a swift lick and discover that her slick cleft is exactly as plump and sweet as I imagined. So is her earthy moan. All of that deserves much more explanation, so I bookmark it for later. Then I lift her into a seated position on the console because we're clearly not making it to any of my bedrooms this go round. My key basket jumps. The lamp wobbles. She obligingly spreads her legs and uses my boxers to pull me into position before eagerly shoving them down. Once they clear my hips, I let them drop to the floor and kick them away, savoring the greedy way she kneads my ass. Not to mention the unmistakable gleam of appreciation as she studies my dick, gives her lower lip a sexy little bite and then flicks her gaze up to mine and stares me dead in the face.

"I can't wait."

As if the sight of her spread out in front of me, flushed, ready and eager, isn't enough to light a fire under my ass.

I lunge sideways, find my wallet and fumble my way to my emergency condom. I'd categorize this as the biggest emergency of my life. I rip the thing open with my teeth and somehow manage to roll it on with my trembling hands. Then, maintaining eye contact, I grab her hands, plant them firmly on the console behind her to make sure she's braced, take her hips and yank her closer. Ever helpful, she tightens her thighs around my waist. I enter her in one sharp thrust that makes us both cry out as though we've been shocked by the same bolt of electricity.

I tense as my head falls back and the pleasure washes over me in suffocating waves. She arches into me, imprinting my chest with the hard points of her nipples as her eyes roll closed. Her body is the absolute perfect fit for mine, made by the universe with me in mind. She's snug. Hot. Creamy. If only I could grow another set of hands or two, I'd gladly hang on to her voluptuous thighs, ass, jiggling breasts and swinging hair at the same time. As it is, I hold her close with one arm and plant the other hand on the mirror behind her to support myself. I note with passing interest that the guy in the mirror bears no resemblance to the man I shaved with this morning. *This* guy? He looks as though he's in pain, with a flushed face, grimacing mouth and eyes like the possessed.

But I am possessed, aren't I? I've been possessed since the day I met her.

I begin to move in strokes that are focused and sharp. Relentless. She seems to like it, judging from her enthusiastic noises. When I find a spot that makes her yell a little bit louder, I stick to it. I take a fistful of her hair and pull it. I duck my head, find the sensitive tendon where neck meets shoulder and bite it. She squeals. Laughs. Frees up a hand to smack me on the ass.

The guy in the mirror is sweaty and red-faced now, clearly circling a heart attack if he continues at this rate for much longer. But I can't stop. Can't hold her tight enough. Can't fuck her hard enough. Can't get enough of her scent, the feel of her or her absolute abandon.

Most of all, I can't shake the feeling that today, with her, I'm experiencing something profound. Becoming part of something extraordinary. And that maybe there was a secret part of me that knew it would be like this with Ally the second I saw her in those yellow scrubs.

She digs her short nails into my left butt cheek as she tenses, and her cries reach a high-pitched crescendo. The sound, naturally, gives me the minute push I need to soar off the cliff with her. Ecstasy slams through me, taking my breath with it as it goes. I stiffen and shout her name roughly a thousand times. I make sure to tighten my hold around her waist, because I need something to anchor me to earth as the pleasure takes over. I keep my face pressed to her neck, riding it out and murmuring God knows what to her in broken syllables.

And when I finally catch my breath enough to open my eyes and raise my head, I'm startled to see all the wild exuberance on the face of that guy in the mirror. The tears in his eyes? That's more like it. Because this kind of unreasonable joy on the heels of a divorce is the most terrifying thing imaginable. And I already know that the excruciating pain I experienced when my marriage collapsed will seem like a bee sting compared to what I'll feel if things with Ally don't work out.

12

ALLY

"I'M JUST GOING TO, ah, run to the bathroom."

The sound of Dr. Jamison's—*Michael's*—husky voice in my ear catches me by surprise. I haven't quite caught my breath yet, nor have the aftershocks completely subsided. I'm floating in that glorious postcoital void where your body feels as though it consists entirely of glittering golden butterflies. My legs have taken possession of Michael's waist and seem reluctant to let him go. Similarly, my throbbing pussy, satisfied though she is at the moment, isn't fully prepared to say goodbye to his stellar dick.

On the other hand, my ass is starting to throb from sitting on the hard console, and I'm sure he's ready to ditch the condom. So I release him from my death grip down below and unwrap my arms from his broad shoulders.

He pulls free and steps back, keeping his head ducked as he runs his hands over his face and through his rumpled hair before turning away. I watch him, wanting to say something airy and unconcerned. The

kind of thing that *Cosmopolitan* magazine teaches sophisti-
cated twenty-first-century women to say after illicit
encounters like the one we just shared. Unfortunately,
that orgasm, a rare and perfect ten out of ten on the
sexual Richter scale, swept my entire vocabulary out of
my brain as it exited my body, leaving me silent and
ridiculous.

I feel particularly naked and vulnerable with the two
halves of my ruined dress framing my body.

Until he hesitates and comes back in for a lingering
kiss on my overheated cheek.

"Be right back," he says.

I lean into the kiss, cupping his cheeks to keep him
close because it's been a lengthy two seconds since I
touched him and I'm now fully addicted. Then I let them
go, keeping him in sight until he disappears down the
long hallway.

By now, my ass is threatening to disown me if I don't
hop down from the console. So I do, wobbling as my feet
hit the ground. My knees have gone spongy, which is no
surprise. Neither is the sweet ache between my thighs.

What *is* a surprise? The fact that I'm facing the elevator, through which anyone could conceivably have
appeared while we were just doing the nasty. I remind
myself that swanky apartments like this one probably
keep these private elevators locked, but still. I'd rather
not test my theory. I take the two halves of my dress and
try to use the belt to reconnect them as I turn to face the
mirror, and that's when the real fun begins.

Holy shit.

That woman in the mirror looks as though she's been
well and truly fucked.

Glowing face. Luminous eyes. Swollen lips. Smeared

makeup. Breasts spilling over the lopsided strapless bra. Erect pink nipples. The console thankfully blocks the lower half of my body. Otherwise, I'm sure I'd be treated to the sight of my juices glistening on my thighs and engorged vajayjay. And the unfiltered view of my extra twenty pounds. So I guess that's a mercy. As for my curly hair, it's such a disaster from his hands that I experience the wild thought that it would be best to just shave it all off and start fresh with a bald head.

My dress is ruined. My panties are gone. And ruined. I have no idea how I plan to get myself home in this condition.

A bubble of wild laughter surges up my throat and out. There's no way to stop it. I don't even try.

What now, Ally?

No. Freaking. Idea.

All I know is that an hour ago I was Bruce's girlfriend, a woman who had an inconvenient but semimanageable crush on her boss.

Now? I have no idea who or what I am or what Michael and I are.

Well, except for shell-shocked.

I am definitely *shell-shocked*.

Because I don't understand how I got here with the Sphinx, a man whose feelings were clearly much more impenetrable to me than I ever imagined. Nor do I get what he did to my body, but it was a million times more intense than I ever dreamed. And that abandoned performance from me on the console just now? Bruce couldn't have achieved that from me if he'd shown up with an annotated copy of the *Kama Sutra*, a box full of sex toys and Chris Hemsworth for backup.

What now, Ally?

How will you act normal at work tomorrow?

Approaching footsteps divert me from trying to answer those questions. I take a deep breath and turn in time for Michael's final approach.

Now wearing a fresh T-shirt and shorts, he's got his arms full. But I'm much more concerned about his expression. His color is high. There's something turbulent in his glittering eyes that I can't quite decipher. And he seems hesitant. A detail I find strangely reassuring.

"Hey," he says quietly.

"Hey," I say, heat rising over my cheeks.

Staring ensues. His heated attention runs down the length of my body and back up again. Hair. Face. Boobs. Pussy. Thighs. Feet. He sees it all. I'm convinced that there's not a follicle of hair on my head or freckle on my body that escapes the intensity of that gaze. Meanwhile, I note the persistent bulge in the front of his shorts. His muscular legs and nice feet. My heart skitters accordingly.

"I, ah, brought you some stuff," he says.

"I see that. What's all this?"

"Just some, ah, water." He passes me a bottle. "A pair of my silk boxers and a washcloth. And one of my, ah, robes."

"You're very thoughtful," I say, touched.

He cocks a brow in the wry expression I love so much. The one that infuriates me half the time. "I am the soul of consideration. Here."

He sets the washcloth on the console and helps me slip the remnants of my dress off. Then he makes a great show of folding and smoothing the ruined fabric before carefully placing it on the bench. I laugh and step into the boxers. When I straighten, he holds the robe open for me as I slide it on. I start to reach for the belt, but he brushes my hands aside and ties it for me.

I watch him, mesmerized by the focus on his down-turned face as he gets the knot exactly the way he wants it. I've seen this focus before, of course. In surgery. But seeing it now really does something to me.

It occurs to me that I need to be careful here. Otherwise, I'm going to wake up one day and discover that I've fallen hopelessly in love with this man. And it'll be way too late for me to do anything to stop it.

"There," he says, looking me in the eye again. "How's that?"

I quickly face the mirror, startled by the delicious intimacy of the moment. "I look good," I say, striking a runway pose. "I think this look will be a big hit when I walk home."

We laugh together, our gazes connecting in the mirror as he comes to stand behind me. I could live and die in that moment. But then the laughter fades and he steps closer, pressing the front of his body up against the back of mine. Heat flares between us again. It doesn't take much on my end, especially when his semi-erection presses against my ass. He slings a possessive arm low across my hips, making a shudder of renewed desire ripple through me. Then he closes his eyes and presses a fervent kiss to the side of my head, right where my hair explodes into a bird's nest. But he doesn't seem to mind. He seems...shaken. In a good way.

Then he raises the lids on those amazing blue eyes again and smiles just enough to make his sexy crow's-feet and dimples pop.

"First of all, you're not going home anytime soon.

Second, do I need to apologize for anything that's happened tonight?"

I think about my ruined dress and underwear. My ruined relationship with Bruce.

"Fuck no. So you're sorry?"

His smile dissipates, leaving him unsmiling and serious as he stares at me with all that heat. "Fuck no."

I can't breathe when he looks at me like that.

I really can't breathe.

"Good," I say, reaching for the water bottle and then unscrewing it for a much-needed sip. I'm going to need to stay well fed and hydrated if I want to keep engaging on the playing field with *this* one. "Then we're on the same page."

"We're *definitely* on the same page."

The purr of satisfaction in his tone makes me feel like the sexiest woman alive. "So…what now?" I ask, hoping whatever it is involves his bed.

"How about I show you my apartment?"

"Let's go," I say, nicely diverted. I've never dated anyone with this kind of money before. Never been to a building like this. I can't wait to see more of his natural habitat.

"This way," he says, taking my hand as though it's the most natural thing in the world.

Our hands fit together as beautifully as our bodies just did. I try to play it off as we take a step or two down the hallway, as though I always feel the zing of a connection like this and there's therefore nothing to see here. But he stops and frowns down at our fingers laced together, looking as stunned as I feel by this turn of events.

"Just to be clear," he says slowly, looking up at me again. "I can touch you now. Whenever I want."

I feel a powerful surge of something that feels suspiciously like triumph.

"I hadn't really given it any thought," I say, shrugging and trying not to smile as we continue down the hallway. "Can I get back to you tomorrow?"

"Tomorrow?"

"I don't like to rush into things."

"Ah."

Without a word, he raises my hand and sucks my middle two fingers deep into his mouth. The delicious suction causes me to cry out. To squirm and melt. I'm not kidding when I tell you that I think that a finger-gasm is and/or should be a thing.

He knows it, too, the cocky SOB. He takes all the time in the world about letting my fingers slide free, eyes gleaming with amusement.

"Tomorrow's too late for me," he murmurs.

"I'll see if I can get you emergency authorization," I say breathlessly.

"Do that," he says, steering me to the right. "Kitchen."

Crazed with desire as I am, it takes me a moment to blink and focus on what I'm seeing. Then the amazing river views on two sides come into focus, giving the impression that his apartment is sailing down the Hudson River. I gasp. The skyline twinkles, further adding to the scene's magic. Inside the kitchen, he's got marble everything. Insane appliances. One of those refrigerators that's built into the cabinets.

"Oh my God," I say, turning in a circle to take it all in. "This is amazing."

"You like?"

"I usually prefer a little more linoleum in my kitchens, but this isn't bad."

"You cook?" he asks, grinning.

"I'm an excellent cook," I say, running my hand over the cool white countertop.

"So am I." Taking my hand again, he leads me to the living room area with its sunken sectionals and gorgeous art on the walls. "Best dish?"

"A roast chicken dinner that'll make you see God. You?"

"Chicken vindaloo. I keep hearing rumors that Michelin wants to give me a star for it."

"I can hardly wait," I say, laughing.

"We can take turns. As long as you agree to clean up on my nights. Living room."

"Deal," I say, trying to match his nonchalance. But it's hard not to squeal at the implication that we'll be spending that much time together. I don't know if he noticed that we just skipped over several intermediate relationship steps, but *I* sure did. "As long as you don't make a huge mess."

"I don't believe in messes. You like the leather?"

"I love the leather. You've done a great job decorating for someone who hasn't been here that long."

"I enjoy it. Trying to make the house a home."

"And are you enjoying your newfound wealth?"

"Absolutely. But the downside to suddenly having a lot of money is realizing that there are empty spaces that money can't fill."

The sudden poignancy catches me by surprise. "You have empty spaces?"

"Things are looking up in that area," he says quietly, giving me a pointed look.

"Good." I have a tough time stopping myself from simpering, but I manage somehow and return to my perusal of his place. "It's quite a house."

"Don't get too impressed. The other rooms aren't done yet. Matter of fact, I'm checking out furniture for my home office this weekend."

"You can't neglect the home office," I say, engrossed in his selection of coffee table books about architecture and design.

"You free? We could grab lunch after."

I look up from the books, again trying to be a cool customer and not lapse into idiotic grinning. Hard to do when I know those keen eyes don't miss anything. But if he wants me here, I plan to be here.

"My weekend is suddenly wide open," I say.

To my surprise, a shadow crosses his expression. "Tell me about, ah, Bruce," he says quietly. "Was that tough?"

I hesitate, debating how much to tell him. But if we're starting something tonight, I want to start it on the right foot. "Yes. I wanted to tell him this weekend, but he called while I was still at the bar. He could hear it in my voice."

"Does he know about me?"

"Yes."

A grim nod. He opens his mouth. Closes it. Tries again. "Are you sad?" he finally asks.

This time there's no hesitation. "Not even a little bit. I mean, I'm sad I hurt him, but it was an easy decision. Because it was the right decision." I pause, letting my own words sink in. "Maybe *that's* the sad thing. That it was such an easy decision."

"No regrets?"

"No regrets," I say, and it's all I can do to keep myself from floating away with happiness.

"Good." He reaches for my hand again and reels me in. "Did I mention that I have several bedrooms here? With beds?"

All the nerve endings in my body prickle to life again, right on cue. "That sounds promising. Do tell."

"*My* bedroom, for example, has a giant bed—"

A bell chimes, startling us.

"That's my sister with your clothes," he says, turning me loose and heading for the hallway. "Hang tight."

"Your *who* with my *what*?" I call after him, trying to get up to speed.

"I called my sister. Asked her to bring you some clothes."

13

ALLY

"WHAT?" I cry. While I certainly appreciate his kind gesture, I'm mortified to discover that his *sister*, whom I've barely met, now knows all about our sexual exploits. And that he seems supremely unconcerned by the whole debacle. "What did you tell her?"

"Don't worry," he says, disappearing around the corner. "She's very discreet. And she knows about you."

"She *knows about me*?"

"Unfortunately. I've never been able to slip anything past her. She picked up on the way I looked at you the day you met her. She'll give me plenty of shit about it, but she'll be discreet. Be right back," he says, heading off. "Make yourself at home."

"But —"

He's already gone, leaving me to frantically tighten the belt around my robe and fret about the opinions his sister may or may not be forming about me right this very second. True, I have no idea where my relationship with Michael will go from here. And true, we're all theoretically grown adults who have sex. I'd just prefer that

Michael's sister didn't know we had *fresh* sex. Like, minutes ago.

Ah well. Nothing I can do about it now.

I'm glumly wondering if there's any liquor nearby and checking the nearest cabinet when I hear the unmistakable sound of the elevator doors whooshing open.

"That was fast," comes the low rumble of Michael's voice. "Appreciate it."

I freeze, forgetting all about the drink. It's not that I want to listen, mind you. It's just that the apartment has Carnegie Hall-worthy acoustics, and I haven't yet figured out how to click my ears off.

"Well, this is another fine mess you've gotten yourself into," Mia replies cheerily.

"Let's do this without the commentary," he says.

"Not a chance. If you drag me over here on an emergency clothes errand, you're going to get commentary. That's just how your world works."

His resigned sigh comes through loud and clear. "Fine. Get it all off your chest."

"So what happened?" she says gleefully.

"We had a minor, ah, snafu. Spilled some wine."

"Really?" she says with laughter dripping from her voice. "Not so minor if the wine managed to rip her dress like this. But some of those Zinfandels pack a punch."

I cringe and cover my hot face with my hands.

"I'll take that," he says with infinite patience. I picture him snatching my dress back from her and replacing it on the bench. "Anything else?"

"So how's *your* night been?" she says, laughing now.

"No complaints," he says, and the trace of smugness in his deep voice does tingly things to my insides, let me tell you.

"I'm so happy for you," she says. I picture her hopping with excitement or giving him a hug. "You finally got your dream girl. And I really like Ally. I think she'll be great for you."

"Thanks."

I find the husky note that creeps into that last word oddly touching, but my mind has shifted to yet another new and head-spinning development tonight, and that gets all my attention.

His dream girl, she said.

Ally, she said.

Which means that...

Wait, what does that mean? More than her noticing a vibe between us in the ER, that's what. That he spoke about me to his sister before tonight? That his feelings about me were strong enough to compel him to do that? That's wonderful. Thrilling.

On the other hand...

On the other hand, I've spent a large portion of the last several years trying to talk myself out of thinking that Michael had any feelings for me at all. A lot of time thinking I was wrong when I was right from the beginning.

A lot of time feeling as though I were crazy.

I turn away from whatever they're saying now and wander deeper into the kitchen, because I don't want to hear anything else. I just heard more than enough to process, and I'm not sure how I feel about it.

Bewildered? Upset is too strong a word. Maybe just...unsettled. I'm not sure whether I can trust Michael and, worse, whether I can trust my own instincts.

I need a minute to think. And a bathroom break.

Since I don't dare go anywhere near the hallway

right now, I head up the back staircase, which is the kind of spiral number that you see in *Architectural Digest* and the local firehouse. Another long hallway with rooms spinning off leads to his bedroom, which is the only one with the lights on. It's no surprise that the room is as darkly masculine and elegant as the rest of the place, with a massive bed that could easily sleep a family of six. I visit the bathroom, studiously avoiding my reflection as I wash my hands and splash water on my face. By the time I return to the bedroom, he's coming in from the hallway.

"There you are," he says, looking pleased with himself as he hands me a shopping bag from Neiman Marcus. "The left side of the bed is mine, by the way. The right-side nightstand is empty, whenever you need to leave anything here."

A nightstand. He's offering me a *nightstand*. It took three months for Bruce to authorize me to leave my toothbrush on his counter.

"Okay," I say, my head spinning. "Thanks."

"Mia brought you a dress and some panties. So you won't have to wear my robe home when you—" He takes a good look at my face for the first time, his expression falling. "What's wrong?"

"Nothing," I say, largely because I don't know how to characterize it myself. I peer into the bag and discover a pretty maxi dress that matches my eyes before setting the bag on the bench at the end of the bed. Mia's got good taste. "You're so thoughtful. Thank Mia for me."

He goes very still, reminding me of the forbidding man I met on the first day of my internship. The man I didn't know at all. Which makes me wonder how well I think I know *this* man. But I recognize reproach when I see it.

"Ally. Don't do that."

I hesitate, thrown off-kilter by his use of my first name, then plunge ahead with my thoughts only partially formed. A practice that usually ends badly for me.

"I just... I'm not quite sure how we got here."

"Neither am I," he says, his expression softening.

"I'm a little shell-shocked."

"So am I. But it's all good."

I start to smile, feeling reassured. But then I remember what I overheard. "I caught part of your conversation with Mia."

"Okay...?"

"She knows about me. I mean, she knew about me before tonight. She knew about me when I met her."

"She did," he says, watching me closely. "She figured out you were the woman I'd told her about."

"So you'd mentioned me to her before."

"I had."

I nod, trying not to sound too overblown about the whole thing. "I kind of feel like she knows more about our relationship than I do."

A tinge of amusement from Michael. "I seriously doubt that."

"I always thought that you liked me. I could never shake the feeling."

"You were right."

"I'd catch you looking at me. Or, I don't know, lingering. Always in my line of sight. Always close. Always so many vibes from you. You always seemed like you had something you wanted to tell me."

"Because I did, Ally," he says.

The tenderness in his tone fires me up. "Yeah, but you acted like you didn't. You pretended it was all in my head. I was obsessed with you. I was falling in love with you. That was the most miserable year of my life, working so closely with you and never saying anything about it. I didn't want to have feelings for a married man, but I couldn't help it. And I kept thinking that I *wasn't* crazy. That I *wasn't* imagining things. Then when I finally worked up the nerve to tell you about it that night in the bar, you pushed me away. You were brutal about it. You *gaslit* me." I bark out a laugh that's shaky and humorless. "And you were really good at it."

"That was the hardest thing I've ever done."

"Which?" I ask bitterly. "There were so many layers to your brilliant performance."

He hesitates, a muscle pulsing in his temple. I notice, for the first time, the tightness of his jaw and the flash of turbulence in his eyes. "All of it."

"Yeah, well, thanks to you, I don't know whether I can trust you or myself."

"I had to, Ally," he says gruffly.

"That's my point." I can't stop my voice from rising. "You *didn't*."

"Well, what did you want me to do?" he shouts, his mouth twisting. "Cheat on my wife and fuck up *your* life in the process? I'm not that guy. You should be glad I'm not."

"Of *course* I didn't want you to cheat on your wife," I say, but that's not entirely true. There were points along the way during that tortured year when I would've happily helped him break his marriage vows. When I lived for the opportunity. Prayed for it. If he'd given me the slightest opening, I would've dived through it. I was that far gone. "I just wanted you to be honest about your feelings. Like *I* was."

"That would've been cheating on my wife," he roars. "Don't pretend you don't understand that. I resisted temptation, which is what any spouse deserves. I gave my marriage *everything* I had to give. I gave until it hurt. When it didn't work out, that had nothing to do with you. Now I have a clean conscience and zero regrets. And you and I both have clean hands."

"That's wonderful for you," I say, close to tears now as I glare him down. "Congratulations on your perfect conscience. Well done. I just want you to know that I cried over you, more than once. I was depressed, because of *you*. That's why I needed that leave of absence. Because you and your whole uninterested routine really hurt me."

"I hurt *myself*!" he says, his voice booming off the walls as he sweeps his arms wide. "You think that was easy? Pushing you away? I knew I was hurting you. I didn't want to hurt you any worse."

"Well, thank God for *that*."

"You think that didn't eat my guts out? You think I didn't want to be with you?"

"Yeah! That's *exactly* what I think! Because that's how you made it look!"

He stiffens and shakes his head, deathly calm now. "You're wrong. Let me assure you."

"If you say so," I say, wavering but not quite ready to believe or forgive him.

"Yeah. I say so," he says, taking two aggressive steps and getting in my face. "But I'll clarify things if you need me to. I remember everything you said. Every time you smiled at me. Everything you *wore*."

I blink, some of my defiance wavering in the face of this ferocity.

"The year that you worked for me was torture. Fucking *torture*. And when we went our separate ways, I thought about you every day. For four years. Once the dust cleared on my divorce, I started looking for my opportunity to see you again. I only went to the party on the boat because I figured you'd be there. So you can imagine my disappointment when I realized there was a Bruce in the picture. I wanted to do the right thing. Respect your relationship. But *I* couldn't shake the feeling that *you* were giving *me* vibes. So I manufactured the job to be with you."

"You—*what*?"

"You think it was a coincidence? Such a golden opportunity for us to work together again? You think I just happened to remember the right color to paint the walls in your office and the artwork you like? Really? And don't look at me like that. You're a great doctor. I'm lucky to have you as a professional colleague. I wouldn't have wanted to work with you otherwise. So don't go there."

I choke off what would've been a biting response about not wanting to be the unworthy recipient of his sexual nepotism, reeling from all these revelations and trying to focus in on the important things. He's wanted me as much as I wanted him. This whole time. We're together now and everything is out in the open. That's all that matters.

"Ally." He hesitates, nostrils flaring. "Say something."

"You could have been a little less noble," I grumble.

He ducks his head and rubs the back of his neck,

looking away. "It's not noble to want a woman who's not your wife. I'm not proud of that."

I realize that he feels shame because of me. And I'm not proud of *that*. "I'm sorry."

Rueful smile as he raises his head again. "For what? Being yourself?"

There's no stopping my grin. Or the flaming blush that covers my face.

"There is one thing I'm glad about," he adds.

The husky new note in his voice catches my attention and accelerates my heartbeat. "Yeah?" I ask quietly. "What's that?"

"That our relationship didn't start with lying or cheating. On either side. Agreed?"

"Agreed," I say from the bottom of my heart.

"Good," he says, moving closer. "Come here."

I'm already on my way. We come together in a ferocious hug that causes us to sway back and forth like a hurricane-swept tree. Then he hefts me up just enough to get my feet off the ground before swinging me around and tossing me on the bed.

I bounce and laugh, coming to rest on my back and hastily levering myself up to my elbows so I can untie the robe and get it open. There's something thrilling about being the recipient of all that unleashed power, as though my extra weight is no more troublesome to him than adding a few more florets to a bag of frozen broccoli. The flash of dark intent in his eyes perfectly matches his indistinct rumble as he sweeps his shirt off and his shorts down.

As the newly crowned luckiest woman in the world, I take a moment to savor everything about him as he looms over me. His height. The breadth of his shoulders.

All that honeyed skin and the way it gleams in the subdued lighting. The rippling muscles in every direction. The jutting erection, already long and thick and fully prepared for me.

Sexy, sexy, *sexy*.

He gives me so much to deal with that there's no time for me to be bothered or embarrassed by my fat upper pubic area. No reason for me to worry about arranging my thunder thighs in a more flattering angle. Honestly, with him looking at me like that? It would be a complete waste of time anyway.

"Let's pick up the pace," I say as he leans sideways and fumbles in the nightstand drawer. My inner muscles are already beginning to ripple with gathering desire, and I don't expect this to take long. "We've got a lot of fucking to do to make up for lost time."

"We certainly do." He withdraws a string of condoms and unfurls it. "Do we need these?"

"I'm on the pill and disease-free. Unless you want them as a fashion statement...?"

"That's a negative. And I'm also disease-free."

"Then we have a plan," I say, reaching for him.

This is our second time together, but my first accepting his unyielding weight on my body. My first absorbing all this direct skin-to-skin heat. Rubbing my swelling nipples against his chest the way I want to. Cocking my hips for him.

The sensations are absolutely exquisite, I must say.

He reaches between us, opening enough space to grip that big dick and run it between my legs, spreading my juices. A single hard thrust and he's inside. *Home.*

"Ah, *Michael*," I say helplessly, arching into him. My legs know what to do without any conscious direction from me, drawing in and wrapping tight around his thighs as he begins to move. Same thing with my arms around his neck and my fingers tunneling through his thick hair. I inhale the fresh cedar scent of him, already intoxicated. "Never stop."

"Deal," he says, picking up the pace as his lips cover mine.

I don't know where he learned to fuck like this, and I don't care. All I know is that every swivel is perfectly timed and expertly placed, hitting my sweet spot over and over again. Being with him like this makes me crazed and loud. This is not the kind of pleasure that can stay politely inside my mouth. It demands to be let out into the world. Funny how I just begged him to never stop when *I'm* the problem here.

When he possesses me like this? I can't come hard enough or fast enough for him.

I scratch his back as I come in a wave of toe-curling ecstasy. I gasp and cry his name. I stiffen and shudder and absorb *his* cries in my mouth as he hurtles off that cliff with me. I sail into a black velvet oblivion and drift back to earth with a body that feels as though it's shimmering with diamonds. And then I snuggle close, happier than I ever thought it was possible to be.

"I have a question for you," I say drowsily a few seconds later, after I've had the chance to recapture most of my breath.

He raises his head from my neck and stares down at me, his hair rumpled and his expression open and relaxed. Warm. "What, angel?"

I smile because I like the sound of that. Then I take his beloved face between my hands, savoring the prickly feel of his beard.

"Were you with me that night? When I had the concussion?"

His eyes crinkle at the corners, lighting up until I feel as though I'm staring directly into the sun. "You know I was."

Yeah. I do.

I pull him in for another kiss, my euphoria tinged with despair. I'm only fooling myself if I think I'm not already hopelessly in love with this man. I can only pray that he does or will eventually feel the same way.

Otherwise, I'm completely screwed. And there's no getting around it.

A MIRACULOUS TWIST of fate allows me to both enjoy lunch at lunchtime for once and to snag an empty table under a market umbrella at the hospital's pavilion next to the café. It's not too hot on this early September afternoon. The sun isn't too bright. My table provides a great view of the koi pond and waterfall. Further proof that all is right with my world, I decide, grinning at no one in particular as I unload my grilled ham and Swiss, chips and cupcake from my tray and sit down. Although, to be fair, any grinning I do these days is a direct result of the presence of one Dr. Ally Harlow in my life for the last several weeks rather than, say, the chirping birds or the availability of red velvet when it comes to dessert selections.

I catch myself scanning the crowd for any sign of her gold-streaked hair, which I know is stupid and futile. First, because I just saw her a couple of hours ago at the office and woke up with her this morning before that. Second, because I checked the board before I came down here and know that, unless her rhinoplasty patient bit the dust in the middle of the procedure, she's still in surgery. Finally, because she would've texted me so we could eat together if she were free.

So I'm doomed to a solitary lunch, which is fine. My disappointment that she's not here knocks the perfection of my day down from one hundred percent to ninety-nine percent. I think I can manage.

Why?

Because I'll see Ally tonight. And tomorrow. And the day after that. And all the days into my immediate future. Which means that I am *happy*, a word that I don't think I've used to describe myself since Santa left the latest electronic gadget under my Christmas tree when I was a kid.

Thanks to Ally? I am unbelievably, ridiculously and perfectly *happy*.

Much to my surprise.

Not that I didn't know that Ally and I would make a great team. I always had that gut feeling. It's just that I never knew I could feel like *this*. Between all my medical training and the years spent trying to do the impossible and save a failing marriage, I've spent a lot of time with big chunks of my life out of whack. Back when I was in med school during my residency, I had a negligible personal life and didn't care because I was so invested in my training. There was a brief period of domestic harmony when my ex-wife and I started dating and got married, quickly followed by misery and workaholism. I started to breathe again and slowly got my shit together once we made the decision to split.

And now…

I don't even know how to put it other than to call it liposuction for my soul. I feel as though I've excised all the bloated, heavy and unhealthy parts and now can breathe again. There's room for relaxation, laughter and enjoyment.

For once in my life, there's nothing missing. No gaping holes.

With Ally? There's passion. Friendship. Peace. Beyond my wildest dreams.

And that, sports fans, is what scares me.

I frown down at my sandwich, picking up the first half. Things could still go south on me here. I've seen this movie before. I know how it could end. There's always a honeymoon period starting out. Everyone's on their best behavior. No one sees the chips in the paint. I'm trying not to be too fatalistic about our relationship. I want to just enjoy this time with her for as long as it lasts without putting any expectations or limitations on it. But it's like swimming in the ocean. You might be having a great day at the beach with your surfboard, catching waves and enjoying snacks and a brew. But there could be something out there, skimming just below the surface and waiting for the perfect opportunity to take you off at the knees.

There's always something out there.

What if Ally decided she didn't want to be with me, for example? Even the idea is like an injection of wet concrete into my veins. I don't think I could—

"Here he is," calls someone, snapping me out of my doomsaying. "Over here, Jake."

I glance up in time to see the final approach of Liam and Jake carrying their lunch trays. I automatically gird my loins and do my best to stifle an eye roll. Are they my best friends and loyal business partners? Absolutely. Would any one of us die for the other two? Without

question. These are the best guys I know. That doesn't
mean that they're not idiots who should immediately be
written into the plot of *It's Always Sunny in Philadelphia*.
I'm sure they'd fit right in with Charlie, Dennis and the
rest of the gang. Although I suppose that makes me Mac.
Something about having seen them once come to actual
blows over whose turn it was to wash the dirty dishes
stacked in the sink back when we were at NYU
precludes me from thinking of them as contributing
members of society.

"Why have you been avoiding us, Mike?" Liam
continues. "You don't call. You don't write. What should
we make of that?"

"That I've had my quotient of morons for the
month?" I say. I hate to go in hard like that right out of
the gate, but I'm eager to divert the conversation away
from my disappearing act ever since Ally and I got
together.

"Harsh," Liam says good-naturedly as he grabs a
chair from the nearest table and slides it over. "What's
with the face when we walked up? Lose another
patient?"

"All my patients are still alive, Liam," I say as the two
of them sit down and offload their trays.

"That'll change," Liam says. "Glad *you're* still alive.
Wish you'd learn to juggle your relationship *and* your
friends—like *I* have—but you can't have everything. It's
probably hoping too much to think that you could walk
and chew gum at the same time. That's why you can't
meet us for drinks or have us over to watch a game or
anything. But hey, as long as you're happy."

"That I am," I say cheerily.

He picks up his fork, stirs his salad and takes a closer

look at *my* lunch. Without a word, he drops his fork again, snatches the sandwich half out of my hand and takes a healthy bite. "Ham and Swiss. Sweet."

"Help yourself," I say sourly.

"Thanks," he says, snatching the remaining half from my plate.

Shaking my head, I slide his salad plate over and get busy with it. That's what happiness will do for you. I can't even get upset. Although I do draw the line at French dressing. "Get blue cheese next time," I tell him.

"Aye, cap."

Jake, meanwhile, grabs his spoon and gives his bowl of clam chowder a morose stir. I'm about to ask what the hell his problem is when Liam flashes his phone in my face.

"Check it out. My new baby."

It's a photo of him and my sister leaning against the latest-model Porsche SUV. I'm impressed despite myself and can't stop my brows from shooting up. One of the benefits of the three of us making our fortunes on the sale of our medical equipment is that we get to enjoy a few perks and toys. We also try to outdo each other in the car and apartment arenas. I'd hoped that my high-end Tesla would keep me in the winner's column for a bit longer, but obviously now I'll have to up my game.

"Not bad," I say.

"Mia had hers first. I fell in love with it. It's a great car. Three hundred and twenty-five horses. Your little Tesla gets, what? Thirty?"

"Ha. Clever." I'm reaching for my water bottle when inspiration strikes. All this talk about cars reminds me that Ally is still tooling around in her old Camry. The car's in good shape and Camrys last forever, but I'd love to see her in something sturdier for driving around the city. Especially with winter coming. In three months.

But still. You can never be too safe. Not when you've got such precious cargo on board.

Would a car be too much for her birthday? Or maybe when she finishes her residency?

And hang on, when *is* her birthday? That's the sort of thing I should know by now. I'd better ask HR when I go back after lunch. Anyway, definitely something to bookmark for later rumination.

"I'm thinking about a Range Rover," I tell him.

"Good choice," Liam says.

I turn my attention to Jake, whose expression looks as though it's been flattened by a steamroller. "What's *your* major malfunction, Jake?"

Hearing his name, he blinks and looks up from his soup with what appears to be great difficulty. I get the feeling that he'd forgotten we were there and hoped we'd have the decency to leave him the fuck alone.

"There's no malfunction," he says, his tone surly. "Nothing to see here. Let's move on."

This, obviously, is tossing bloody chum into shark-infested waters. I circle back around for a closer look.

Jake is hollow-eyed and thin-cheeked, the kind of haunted look that only ever has one source.

"Who is she?" I ask.

"The nanny," Liam says with unrestrained glee.

"The *nanny*," I say, leaning in because shit just got interesting. "I didn't even know there was a nanny."

"That's why you need to stay in touch," Liam says, polishing off the first half of my sandwich and starting in on the second. "You miss out on important news. Like when one of your best friends runs his personal life into the ground."

"Can we not?" Jake asks.

"He fucked the nanny," Liam says, ignoring this plea. "Now he's trying to keep his hands off her. It's not going well. As you can see."

Jake glares across the table at Liam with murder in his eyes. "I didn't fuck her as the nanny. Matter of fact, let's watch our language around this whole subject."

Liam and I exchange sidelong looks and do our best not to burst into wicked laughter. Jake's got it much worse than we suspected, which means that he is now ripe for roasting. This is *great*.

"She and I met on a dating app. We, ah, hooked up. Next day, guess who shows up when it's my turn with the kids?" Jake shudders at the memory. "My ex hired her."

"Oh, shit," I say, abandoning all efforts to hide my amusement.

"Exactly," Jake says, tossing his spoon down. Leaning back in his chair, he runs his hands over the top of his head and curses. He discovers that one of his knees is jiggling and rubs his thigh to make it stop. Then he looks at us with desperation in his eyes. "I can't stop thinking about her. I'm dying to fuck her again."

Liam and I exchange a blank look.

"So?" I say.

"You're not this stupid, Mike," Jake says. "First of all, she's my employee. Second, the kids love her, and I don't want to screw that up. Third, Marlene would kill me."

"Well, that's true," Liam says darkly. "Marlene's a *nightmare*."

Liam and I never liked Marlene. One of the happiest days in the life of our friendship with Jake was the day he decided to divorce her.

"So what are you going to do?" I ask quickly. Jake is still looking as though he might lunge across the table for Liam's neck, and I don't have time to bail anyone out of jail today. I've got surgery this afternoon.

"No fucking idea," Jake says with a resigned sigh as he picks up his spoon again.

"Well, you'd better be careful," Liam tells him with a pointed glance. This clown. Ever since he got his relationship with my sister straightened out, he thinks he's a romantic Gandhi or Buddha. All wisdom, all the time. "Otherwise, you wind up like me or Mike here."

"What the fuck does that mean?" I ask, startled to hear myself lumped in with a guy who's engaged.

Liam holds up his left hand and, without a word, points to his ring finger.

I recoil involuntarily. I've been divorced for a year now, but the wounds haven't quite healed all the way over. I'm like a guy who got run over by a bus, lost his leg and started using a prosthetic limb. I've found my footing and am indefinitely on the upswing, yeah, but I'm not quite ready to sign up for a marathon just yet.

"Hang on," I say, putting my hands in stickup position. "Ally and I are just getting to know each other. This is all fresh and new. No one said anything about marriage."

Liam makes a derisive noise. "So *that's* the story you're telling?"

"It's true," I say.

Liam pauses to give me a clinical once-over, as though he's evaluating me for surgery. "Mike's got a classic case of denial," he tells Jake, as though he's brought Jake in for a second opinion. "Poor fool doesn't recognize his own symptoms. He can't live without her for two seconds. He's been scanning the crowd for her this whole time we've been talking."

"I have not—" I begin hotly.

"He spends every night with her," Liam continues. "No longer bothers to hang out with us or even text us back. How many times have we asked him to join us for drinks tonight, Jake?"

"At least two for me," Jake says, happy to throw *me* under the bus if it means he's out of the hot seat.

"Also two for me," Liam says.

By now my face is burning up because they're right. I open my mouth to issue a standard excuse about how busy I am lately and so on and so forth, but Liam holds up a hand to stop me.

"Here she comes now, Jake," he says with unrestrained glee. "Let's see how Mike acts. Maybe we've judged him too harshly. Maybe he's not, in fact, as whipped as we think he is."

Here's where it gets sad, folks.

I *know* they're giving me shit. I *know* I'm currently under their microscope. I know I need to channel my inner Al Pacino as Michael Corleone and act like a cool cucumber. Too bad I can't manage it. My heart rate kicks up. My grin takes off. My head whips around so fast that I can already feel my incipient case of whiplash.

And there she is with a to-go clamshell and drink, her bright smile, shining eyes and gleaming hair the missing ingredients I need to make my soul soar.

"Hey," I say as our gazes connect. I'm already halfway out of my seat to kiss her before I catch myself and play it off by grabbing another chair from a nearby table and pulling it over for her. We've sworn to keep our relationship on the down-low here at the hospital, and I plan to hold up my end of the pact even if it kills me. I, of course, blabbed about her to the fellas in a moment of weakness that I now regret, for obvious reasons, but they'll never tell. "Wasn't sure you'd make it down."

I should mention that something happens to my voice when she shows up. Her presence makes me softer some-how. Tender. Unfortunately for me, the idiots notice. As evidenced by their wicked and poorly concealed grins.

"Neither was I," she says, stopping at the chair but not sitting. "I just wanted to grab some lunch and see the sun for a minute. I can't stay. Sorry to miss this power summit. Looks like the three of you started without me."

Liam and Jake met Ally in passing at the hospital before the two of us got together and have seen her a couple of times in passing since. They all seem to get along like a stack of twenty-year-old newspapers and a lit match, which certainly makes my life easier.

"There's a small fine for being late," Jake tells her.

"Oh, no," she says, laughing.

"It's only a thousand dollars," Jake says. "Don't even worry about it."

"I think special dispensation should be made for the poorest member of the group," she says.

"Sorry," Jake says. "If we bend the rules for you, we have to do it for everybody."

More laughter.

"So listen," Liam tells her, shooting me an evil look. "We were just talking about you. Your ears must be burning."

I stiffen and crank my gaze into veiled-death-strike mode for his benefit.

Swear to God, I don't want to kill one of my best friends. But I will.

"Oh, yeah?" She raises her brows at me. "That sounds interesting."

"Can you let Mike come out and play with us tonight? We've been trying to get him to come for drinks," he says, now sending me a *relax* look.

"You're giving me way more power than I have," she says, blushing.

No, they're not.

"It's not up to me," she continues. "Ask Michael."

"It's not a big deal," I say, looking up at her. See? There goes my voice again. Giving me away. "I wasn't sure if we had anything planned for tonight."

She blinks, but her smile remains firmly in place. "Nothing that can't wait," she says.

My heart sinks. I don't want to have drinks with the Idiot Posse. I want to be with *her* tonight.

"You sure? Sounds like there was something."

"I was just going to make dinner at my place. We can do it another night."

"Perfect. It's all settled," Liam booms before I can tell her that I can do drinks with these two fools another night, which is what I plan to do. "Thanks for being so understanding, Ally."

"No worries," she says, turning to go. "I'll cut you a check on my late fee by the end of next week. How's that?"

"Unfortunately,   there'll   be   a   twenty-percent surcharge on late payments of the late fee," Jake says, shrugging. "It's not personal. Just business."

"Understood," she says, laughing. Then she zeros in on me with a tiny wink that makes my heart thud. "Bye."

"Bye," I say glumly, watching her depart with zero idea whether I'll even get to see her again before I leave at the end of the day.

I want the record to reflect that I let her go without a touch, a kiss or even a knowing glance. I keep my hands to myself and do the right thing, an effort that shaves a year off my life, easy.

My life sucks. Clearly.

Then it gets worse.

"Nope," Liam says. "Mike's not whipped."

"Not at all," Jake adds. "What were *we* thinking?"

"Poor sap. He doesn't even realize that he's already married," Liam says, tapping his temple. "Up *here*. Where it counts."

That hits close to home. A lot closer than I'd care to admit, even to myself.

I scowl to hide my vague feeling of panic about the whole topic.

Meanwhile, my two so-called best friends, who knowingly ruined my night with Ally, break into raucous laughter.

"Fucking assholes," I mutter, kicking off another round of guffawing at my expense.

"THANKS FOR COMING on such short notice," I tell Kelly early that evening, when she arrives at my apartment carrying a bottle of champagne in one hand and balancing a pink cake box from Valentina's on the other. "I wasn't looking forward to celebrating my birthday by myself."

"Are you kidding?" She hurries in and deposits her items, including her enormous Louis Vuitton, on the kitchen counter, then pulls me in for a hug. "Once I heard you were cooking your world-famous chicken enchiladas? Where else would I be?"

"So you're here for the free food and not for the occasion?" I say sourly, trying not to laugh. "Can't say I'm surprised."

She turns me loose and scowls. "It's your own fault. You should've let me take you out to the standard birthday dinner last week when I invited you. But no. You wanted to be with your precious Michael, *who doesn't even know* it's your birthday. That's on you."

"Well, you're right about that," I say glumly.

"This is what happens when you put all your eggs in the man basket," she continues sagely, washing her hands and grabbing the flutes from the cabinet while I check the chicken enchiladas in the oven. "You cuddle up with your new love and make your own little honeymoon bubble. Ignoring friends who wonder what they've done wrong to deserve this kind of dismissive treatment—"

"Here we go," I say, rolling my eyes and bracing myself for the entire speech.

"And now here you are. Sad and pathetic. Desperate for a birthday hug and a piece of cake."

"Thank you for that unsolicited lecture." I get ready to duck as she works on the champagne bottle, but she pops the cork like a pro and doesn't spill a drop. "I don't suppose it matters that I have not ignored you and *you* were the one who canceled our last girls' night."

"Details," she says airily, flapping a hand before she starts pouring. "It's much more dramatic to say that you kicked me to the curb rather than the truth."

"What, that you were too tired and put yourself to bed at eight o'clock that night?"

"Exactly."

We laugh, then she passes me a glass and raises her own in a toast.

"To the birthday girl. May this be her best year ever."

"I'll drink to that," I say, clinking our glasses. "Thanks. Love you."

"Love you too. Oh. Before I forget." She sets her bag on the counter, rummages in the LV and produces…

"Oh my God, a gift basket?" I cry, incredulous. "Are you kidding me?"

"Just a few spa items," she says, looking smug now that she's pulled off her big surprise. "And here's that mask I was telling you about. Makes your face like butter."

"I can't wait." I pull her in for another quick hug and kiss. "Thanks again."

"Anything for you. I was promised snacks. Chips? Guac?"

"Coffee table."

"Let's get this party started."

She puts the champagne on ice while I grab the remote. Then we reconvene on the sofa and study our movie options.

"*Sixth Sense* or *The Cabin in the Woods*?" I ask.

"*Pride and Prejudice*. The Keira Knightley version."

"Not the mood I was going for, but good alternative," I say, about to make the selection. "Let's do it."

"Hang on." Her tone shifts to crisp professionalism, as though she's calling a meeting to order. I brace myself. "How are things with the sexy doctor? Tell me everything."

Unfortunately, there's no way for me to play it cool when the topic turns to Michael and our new relationship. I don't even bother trying. I've resigned myself to my new reality, which is that I've turned into a human mylar smiley-face balloon, floating and bobbing happily through life.

The thing is…

The thing is that I'm re-obsessed with him, and it's every bit as intense as I feared. God, it's so nerve-racking to admit it, even to myself. Especially this early in our relationship, even though we've known each other for a while now. But I am. There's no denying it. Worse, I'm talking about crazy love. Scary love. The kind that leaves you ecstatic and terrified at the same time. I know we're in a honeymoon period where the sex is incredible and the problems are few. Everyone's on his or her best behavior. But I'm a grown woman who's had enough life experience to know the difference between a relationship that shows growth potential (like I had with Bruce) and the kind of synchronistic connection that indicates something rare and precious is happening.

The way we've woven our lives together has been seamless. Effortless. A complete joy.

Why?

I'm no expert, but I think it's because Michael and I *get* each other. It's the looks we exchange when one of us is coming out of surgery and one of us is going in. The quiet understanding with no words needed. The way our opinions align on everything from politics to favorite books (anything James Patterson) to furniture selections. The way we work together at the office. In the OR. In the kitchen when we make dinner together. In bed.

We have the kind of relationship that makes it crystal clear why it never could have worked out between me and Bruce. Or me and any other man, for that matter. I just pray that Michael feels—or one day *will* feel—the same way.

"It's going great," I say, the swoon in my voice coming through loud and clear.

"Really? And the sex?"

"I'm a lucky girl," I say, disappearing behind a sip of champagne in a lame attempt to get myself together.

"That's *wonderful*," she says, hitting me with that sardonic raised eyebrow of hers. The thing is lethal. It should be a banned weapon. "So naturally you decided not to tell him about your birthday."

I blow out a breath and have a tough time defending myself. "I didn't know what to do. We haven't been together that long. I didn't feel comfortable announcing that it was my birthday and then demanding, I don't know, a fancy dinner out or some such. I don't want him to think I'm after his money. Plus, first holidays and birthdays together can be so awkward. You never know what to get. What would *you* have done?"

"That's easy," she deadpans. "Demand the gift."

"Yeah, okay," I say, helping myself to a chip.

"So where is he tonight?"

"Drinks with his friends."

"Hmm," she says thoughtfully, also helping herself to a chip. "I've been meaning to ask you—any word from Bruce?"

My heart sinks at the reminder of the wreckage I've left in my wake. "No. I mean, we've had a couple of texts. I mentioned that. But no real conversation. I'd love for us to be friends at some point, but I think we need the space from each other. And I'm sure he needs a cooling-off period."

"That's probably smart. What about your lease? Didn't you let the apartment go because you thought the two of you would be getting something bigger together?"

"I did," I say grimly. "I'll be moving come November first."

"Where will you go?"

I do my best to look sweet, innocent and low-maintenance. "Your sofa?"

She grimaces. "Not a chance. Our friendship would never survive."

"True."

"I did see that there are some units available in the building on—"

My phone buzzes on the coffee table. The display lights up with Bruce's picture. I gasp.

"It's him," I say.

"Answer it!"

I pick up the phone and hit the button, my heart pounding. "Hey," I say.

"Hey. Am I catching you at a bad time?"

"No. This is perfect," I say, getting up to head into the kitchen and check on the enchiladas. "Just sitting here with Kelly."

"Tell her I said hi."

"Will do."

I hesitate, waiting.

He takes a deep breath. "How have you been?"

"Really good," I tell him. "You?"

"Not so good," he says, and I hear the self-deprecation in his voice.

I feel the hard pinch of guilt. "I'm so sorry, Bruce. I never meant to hurt you."

"I know. But you're with the guy now, aren't you?"

I don't want to answer, but I can't see any way around it. Nor do I want to give him the wrong idea or any false hope. "Yes."

"And you're happy?"

I really wish he'd stop asking these questions. I want to be honest, but there's only so much I can do without rubbing salt on his wounds. I shoot a *help me!* glance at Kelly, who is, of course, riveted to the proceedings. She can't hear the entire conversation, but she shrugs encouragingly anyway.

"It's still early, but…yes," I tell him.

There's a long and painful pause. "Good," he says, his voice tight now. "So, listen. I wanted to wish you a happy birthday."

There goes another little piece of my heart, crumbled into dust. It's not that I want Bruce back. It's just that this confirms my instincts that he's a good guy who will make someone a wonderful husband one day.

"I really appreciate that, Bruce," I say quietly. "Have I mentioned that you're a class act?"

He makes a derisive noise. "Sure I am. Also, I need to get my stuff from your apartment."

I've already packed up his various sweatshirts, toiletries and other small items he left around my apartment. I debated whether to drop them in the mail for him in D.C., but that seemed harsh without discussing it first, kind of like a final *fuck you* to add insult to injury.

"I've got it all in a box for you. I wasn't sure if you'd be coming back to the city anytime soon, but I'd be happy to drop it in the mail?"

"Yeah. Sounds good."

I stifle a huge sigh of relief. I'm not up for another face-to-face with Bruce just yet, so this is ideal. As for him, I can't decide whether he sounds relieved or disappointed.

I plow ahead, determined to overcome some of this awkwardness.

"How are *you* doing? How's work been going? And I've been wondering about your mom's—"

"I just don't get it," he says, sounding pissed now. I tense and send Kelly an *oh, shit!* look, which she returns with interest. Then I give myself a quick mental kick in the ass. I don't know why I didn't hang up after we agreed on the shipping arrangements, ending this conversation before things went south on me. But no. I had to push it *one* step too far. "I'm trying to be a decent guy about this whole thing, but I was in love with you. I wanted to marry you. I would've proposed at Christmas if I'd moved to the city."

I head back to the sofa and collapse, looking up and searching for divine intervention as though it's hidden in the crown molding. But there's nothing.

"I'm really sorry." I clear my throat. "I don't know what to say to that."

"Does any of that matter to you?"

I open my mouth, but there's no answer. None that I want to give, anyway. It matters because it's immensely flattering and humbling to know that he cared about me that much, but there's just no comparison between the way I felt about him and the way I feel about Michael. It's like comparing sequins and flawless diamonds.

"Bruce—"

"You know what? Forget it. I don't know why I'm mentioning it. There's no point. Actually, there is a point. I hope you know what you're doing. I hope you made a good choice. I hope this guy is worth it. Because you and me? As far as I'm concerned, we could've gone the distance. I just...wanted you to know that. Maybe I'm stupid, but I wanted you to know."

This whole speech hits a little too close to home for me. Because only time will tell if I made a good choice with Michael. Not that I'd want to, say, hook up with Bruce again if my relationship with Michael doesn't work out. That would never happen. Bruce isn't the right guy for me, and I see that with a clarity I didn't have before. It's just that my relationship with Michael is fluid and new. While things are clearly going well, I'm not quite sure where I stand or where this is going. To make matters worse, I'll have so much more heartache if I lose Michael now, after having been with him, then I ever had back when I could only fantasize about being with him.

"Forget about me, Bruce," I say quietly. "The sooner you do, the sooner the right woman is going to snap you up. And you'll be so glad when she does."

Longest pause of the night. "That's my plan," he says, his voice hoarse. "Bye, Ally."

He hangs up before I can respond.

I toss the phone away and glance over at Kelly, my heart heavy.

She shakes her head and makes a whole production out of giving me a scathing once-over. "You are one heartless bitch, aren't you?"

I burst into startled laughter. This is one of the best things about Kelly. She always knows the right thing to say at the right time.

"Seriously, don't beat yourself up on your birthday," she continues, shrugging. "You can't help it if you have feelings for someone else. You were honest with Bruce. That's all you can do."

"He says he would have married me."

"That doesn't surprise me."

"He says he hopes Michael is worth it," I add.

She goes all somber on me, which doesn't exactly help calm my nerves over the status of my brand-new relationship with Michael, the man who doesn't even know it's my birthday.

"So do I. I've seen what he can do to you. I don't want to have to pick up the pieces again."

As if I want to be heartbroken and depressed again.

"On *that* happy note, I'm going to need a slice of birthday cake," I say.

"How much time have we got before the enchiladas are ready?"

"Ten or fifteen minutes," I say.

"Oh, yeah," she says, reaching for the pink box. "We're definitely going to need cake to hold us over."

It's nearly midnight by the time she leaves, a point at which I feel my birthday has been thoroughly and successfully celebrated. I send her home with a big slab of Chantilly cake (Valentina's knows what they're doing with the dessert, take it from me) and leftover chicken enchiladas for lunch tomorrow. Then I hit the shower, throw on my favorite T-shirt (it's got boxes for Ms., Mrs. and Miss, with the box for Dr. checked off) and encase my face in Kelly's sheet mask, since I obviously want buttery skin now that I'm a year older.

I wander back to the kitchen and am in the middle of debating the wisdom of another slice of cake and/or a final glass of champagne—I'd need to wash the cake down with *something*—when a knock on my door scares the shit out of me.

I hurry over and check the peephole.

Michael.

My heart soars because I always want to see him.

Then it sinks because I never want him to see me like *this*. I'm a fervent believer in keeping the mystery alive in a relationship.

"I hear you creeping around inside," he says in that wry tone of his. "Are you going to let me in?"

"*No.* I thought you were with the guys tonight."

"We finished up a little while ago."

"Okay, but why would you just show up with no warning? I have a mask on my face."

"News flash: I see you with a mask on your face every day at the hospital."

"No! A mask to give me buttery skin."

"Unnecessary. You already have buttery skin. Are you letting me in, or not?"

"As long as you brace yourself," I say with a resigned sigh as I unlock the door. "I don't want you to be scared."

"*You're* the one who should be scared. Why do I have to discover that *today* is your birthday from the HR person at the office?"

Oh, that. "I wasn't sure what to do," I say, swinging the door open. "I didn't want you to think that— Oh my God. *They're gorgeous!*"

He's got a massive bouquet of red roses nestled in the crook of his elbow, as though he hijacked the local florist's delivery truck on Valentine's Day.

I press a hand to my heart, unspeakably touched by his thoughtfulness. "These are all for *me*?" I squeak.

"Damn, that *is* terrifying," he says, making a show of looking me over as he comes inside. "I thought it was your birthday. Not Friday the thirteenth."

An uncontrollable burst of laughter makes my mask crinkle as I carefully reach past the flowers and cup his face to bring him in for a lingering kiss on his smiling mouth. "Thank you," I say when I let him up for air.

"I did it to save my own ass. I don't want to be in the doghouse for missing my girlfriend's first birthday now that we're together."

Oh my God! He just called me his *girlfriend*!

"Very smart," I say gravely.

"You like the flowers?" he asks, passing them over.

"I *love* the flowers." The moment between us is so delicious and my heart is so full that it seems like the most natural thing in the world to just go with the flow and say what I feel. "And I love you. I'm crazy in love with you."

16

ALLY

SO MUCH FOR drifting through life like a giant smiley-face balloon. His reaction to my heartfelt but ill-conceived confession is to stiffen, the grin slowly sliding off his face. And the effect on me feels exactly as though he's taken an oversized needle, the kind they use in the old Looney Tunes cartoons, and given me a sharp jab with it. Leaving me embarrassed and deflated as the silence stretches into awkwardness.

"Ally…"

"I'm just going to take care of the flowers," I say quickly, turning away as my cheeks begin to burn. I don't know what he's going to say, but if it's an *it's not you, it's me* speech, I need a second to get my mind right. And to get rid of this stupid mask and restore an ounce or two of dignity. "I'll be right back."

I find a vase for the roses, then duck into the bathroom and splash water on my face. Neither of which is easy to do with trembling hands and suffocating dread.

Why didn't I keep my mouth shut? Why can't I just

play the long game where he's concerned, letting him take the lead and hoping he'll get there in his own time? He's an alpha male. I know that. *He* likes to take the lead on things like this. All I needed to do was be patient and give him more than ten minutes for our relationship to develop. Now I've jumped the gun and forced his hand on something he may not have been ready to discuss.

Why? Because I had a moment of euphoria-induced idiocy caused by hearing him call me his girlfriend for the first time. Also because I'm too stupid to live, clearly.

And yet...

It was a relief to let my feelings go so they could fly free. Even if they immediately got banged up and crumpled to the ground like a robin hitting a plate glass window, at least they had their moment of glory.

So?

What now?

I could go back and, I don't know, try to find a graceful way off the playing field by claiming that I got carried away because I was excited about the flowers and had too much champagne with Kelly. But then I'd be a liar. And I discover, much to my surprise, that I don't want to take it back.

I *do* love him. He needs to know. And the two of us need to figure out where we go from here.

I dry my face, square my shoulders, take a deep breath and head back to the living room, where I discover him sitting on the sofa rubbing his hands together with his elbows resting on his knees—wearing the exact same grim expression I've seen him use when he's lost a patient and needs to gear himself up to inform the family.

All Sphinx. No sign of Michael, my tender lover and best friend of the last several weeks.

I hover in the doorway, wishing I thought to throw on some shorts and a bra. I'm feeling way too vulnerable and exposed as it is.

His head comes up. Our gazes connect across the distance of ten feet or so as he hastily stands and faces me. I've never been much good at figuring out what he's thinking, but whatever it is seems to have a healthy portion of turbulence stirred into it. And maybe a flare of panic.

Whatever it is, it's murder on my sinking morale.

"I didn't mean to freak you out," I say before he can open his mouth.

"You didn't."

"Yes, I did. It's all over your face."

He blinks, shoves his hands in his pockets and ducks his head, trying to shutter what I've already seen. I get the feeling that he's searching for words and maybe wishing he could pick some helpful ones up from my sisal rug.

Worse, I get the feeling that he feels stuck and would dearly love to pull the lever on a trapdoor to get him out of here as soon as possible.

"You don't feel the same way," I say dully. "Just tell me."

He glances up again, those eyes cool now. Aloof. And there's a new rigidity in his posture, an invisible force field around him that screams at me to make sure I keep the minimum safe emotional and physical distance between us. As if I'd dare try to sneak closer with him looking at me like *that*.

"I don't know what to say, Ally."

Wow, I think as my mouth twists into an involuntary grimace.

Karma wasted zero time in tracking me down and taking a big bite out of my ass over the whole Bruce thing, didn't she?

"We haven't been together that long," he hurriedly continues. "And it hasn't been that long since my divorce. I didn't see myself moving that quick this fast. I need a minute. That's all."

And there it is, that classic variation on the whole *it's not you, it's me* theme:

I need a minute.

With the writing all over the wall, you'd think I'd be smart enough to shut up and call it a night before things get any worse. But no. I speed ahead like an impatient driver who thinks she can ignore the flashing red lights and zoom across the tracks even though there's a freight train zooming right toward her.

"I hate to break it to you, but we were already moving fast before I opened my big mouth tonight," I say, unable to keep a tinge of bitterness out of my voice. "Maybe a relationship this intense is normal for you, but it's not for me. I assure you."

"I never said that."

"So...you, what? You need a break? You don't love me? You'll never love me?"

"No, Ally," he says, looking stricken. "That's not what I'm saying."

By this point, I'm so upset that I barely hear him.

"I hate that I'm asking you these questions. I hate that I'm being this needy woman," I say, doing my best to keep my growing anguish under wraps. "But I need to know. And you're not doing me any favors if you know I'm not the one for you and you don't tell me."

His mouth opens and his eyes widen. But no words come out for the longest time, which may be for the best. A guy with *that* look of utter paralysis on his face doesn't have anything good to say.

"You're putting words in my mouth," he says. "You're hearing things that I'm not saying."

"Then what are you saying?" I say, dread making my voice thick.

There's another delay while he tries to say the words, almost as though each one is kicking and screaming on the way up his throat and out of his mouth.

"I'm saying it'll be okay. I just need to get there in my own time. When I'm ready."

"When you're ready," I echo faintly.

Not exactly a hearty *fuck you*, but it sure feels like it. Especially after I just joyfully gave him my heart on a silver platter. With sprinkles on top.

At this dismal moment, I'm not exactly in the mood for this lame consolation prize when my own feelings are so clear and intense. What good is a couple of crackers and a dried-out slice of cheddar cheese when you've been hoping for a sumptuous buffet?

Nor am I quite ready to end this conversation.

Even so, this is another opportunity for me to slink away and end the pain before it gets any worse. I'd be a fool not to take it. But the two of us have come so far together, and things with him are a million times better than I ever imagined they would be. I had a good life before. I was satisfied. But with Michael? I don't know how to explain it other than to say he makes my soul feel as though it's glowing with molten gold.

Maybe I'm fatally stupid, but I can't let him go. Not without a bigger fight than this.

I think of all the fun we've shared since we got together and experience more of that unfettered happiness. I'm sure some of this must show on my face as I ease closer and do my best to explain myself in a calm and rational manner.

"Here's the thing," I say quietly. "I'm ready now. I'm a grown thirty-two-year-old woman. I've dated people. I know what I need from a relationship. Which means that I don't need time to figure this out with you. As far as I'm concerned, you don't need a probationary period to earn a place in my life. Because I already know that you're it."

He stares at some distant point past my shoulder, still except for a muscle pulsing in his jaw as the corners of his mouth turn down.

"I'm done with my training now," I say, determined to get it all out before my remaining courage dwindles to nothing. "My career is in a good place. I want a family. I want *kids*. What I don't want to do is waste my time with someone who doesn't feel the same way."

"Understood," he says after an endless silence, still not looking at me.

I blink as those three syllables reverberate through the air, desperately searching for some sign of Michael and finding only the Sphinx with all his barrier walls and razor wire firmly in place.

Wait, what?

Understood?

That's it? I pour my heart out —*again*—and I get an *understood?*

What does that even mean?

"Yeah, okay," I say with a humorless laugh, finally

done with this conversation. "I can't *believe* I was actually going to suggest that we live together when my lease ends."

His head whips back around. *"What?"*

"Just because, I don't know, we've spent every single night together since we became a couple." I take a beat to rein in some of my runaway emotions, because I do *not* plan to cry tonight. "And because I'm obviously not great at reading the room. Anyway, doesn't matter now. Time for you to go."

I march stiffly to the door and swing it open for him.

"I'm not leaving," he barks, hurrying after me. "Not like this. We need to talk."

I am *so* unmoved by this new urgency. "We've talked. Bye."

"We can't go to sleep on something like this, Ally." There's a pleading note in his voice now. A note of desperation. "We need to work it out. I don't want this to ruin your birthday."

My birthday?

He kicks in the rest of my life and he's worried about my *birthday*?

"Good news," I say, making a show of checking my watch before glaring him in the face. "My birthday ended a few minutes ago. Get. The. Fuck. Out."

He looks as though he wants to say something else but wisely thinks better of it. He walks out, ducking his head as he goes.

I slam the door. A childish move, sure, but wildly satisfying.

Then I return to the sofa and cut another huge slab of birthday cake, determined to drown my sorrows in sugar and warm champagne.

I get several bites in with periodic pauses to wipe away angry tears that persist in falling. Icing always helps when your heart's been cracked in two. Check the medical literature. It's a known fact. Even so, oblivion refuses to come. Especially with the sudden reappearance of the painful memory of that night at the bar four years ago. That terrible night when I made another heartfelt confession. And he came back at me with another apathetic and soul-killing response.

My most painful memory, actually. Evidently, it wants to give me the two-fingered salute and rub my face in the fact that I would have seen the writing on the wall if my judgment weren't so fatally compromised when it comes to the good Dr. Michael Jamison.

I'm by myself at a table, where I've been for a while now, considering the relative wisdom of a fifth tequila shot. On the one hand, I've got rounds at the crack of dawn tomorrow and I'm not much of a drinker. Oh, and I'm recovering from a concussion and shouldn't be drinking at all. On the other hand, it would be nice if I could take the edge off the gut-punched feeling I've had for hours, ever since Dr. Jamison told me he didn't visit me the other night when I was in the hospital. The whole interlude was so surreal and disorienting, like those hyper-realistic dreams where you're about to have the best sex of your life with a phantom lover only to wake up at the very last second and realize there's no one in the bed with you at all. And you're left with emptiness and frustration that's so intense it borders on despair.

That's where I am right now.

I could have sworn he was there with me, sitting by my bed. Holding my hand. But it was all a figment of my concussed brain.

Yep. I definitely need another shot.

I signal for the server, tracking her progress as she hurries past my table without acknowledging me in my dire hour of need. That's when I see him sitting alone at a booth against the back wall and gasp.

Dr. Jamison, in his shirt sleeves now, grim-faced as he swirls his drink in its tumbler.

He looks dangerous. This is not a guy you want to interrupt. Nothing about him seems approachable or warm. This is a moody lion in his cage just waiting for the wrong mouse to scurry through the bars.

And I've had just *enough liquid refreshment to look at all that and think,* Hmm, yeah, I've got a few things I need to get off my chest. *A few feelings that won't stay inside another second. Now seems like the perfect time. I'm sure he won't mind.*

So I grab my final shot and head for his table, propelled by my wounded heart and the righteous hand of God to demand answers and justice. He glances up, those dark brows sinking steadily lower over his flashing eyes, and watches as I slide into the seat opposite him and thunk my shot down.

We stare at each other. The crackling air seems so fraught and turbulent that it's like a named hurricane has begun its slow rotation on the table between us.

"You're not drinking shots while recovering from a concussion, are you, Harlow?"

"Nope," I say, blinking to hold back sudden hot tears as I grab said shot and toast him with it. I try to smile but feel it pull to one side, as though my face has gone crooked. "Lemonade."

I maintain eye contact over the rim of the glass as I down it, fascinated to discover that his expression isn't quite so impenetrable after all. He looks as though he wants to smack the glass out of my hand and then throttle me for being so stupid.

That's one thing we can agree on, I guess. Me being stupid.

"I don't feel like talking," he says, his words slow and deliberate. "I feel like sipping my drink in peace so I can unwind before I

grab some carry out and go home. To my wife. Why don't I get you a cab?"

"I see what you did there," I say, all those repressed tears making my voice gravelly. "You reminded me about your wife."

"You're drunk. And babbling."

He's good. I'll give him that. He actually seems bored. Maybe a little annoyed. If it weren't for the slight tremble in his steady surgeon's hand as he reaches for his drink, I'd be convinced he has no idea what I'm talking about.

"The thing is, you don't have to remind me about your wife, Dr. Jamison. She's on my mind. All the time. Because I think she's the luckiest woman in the world."

He freezes, his drink halfway to his lips.

"I'm not proud of myself," I say, resting my elbows on the table and leaning closer because my body finds it hard enough to stay away from him when I'm sober, and damn near impossible when I'm drunk. "I know you're my boss. I know you're married. I don't throw myself at men—"

"Then **don't**," he says before downing his entire drink in a single rough gulp.

"—and I'm so ashamed of myself for doing this. I'm not this person. But you can't keep expecting me to keep it all inside when you know how I feel about you."

"You need to **stop**, Harlow," he says, the hard edge of his voice cutting across the crowd's chatter in the background like a surgeon's blade. "Before we both regret it."

"I can't," I say, agonized. "Aren't you listening? That's my point. I can't stop thinking about you. I can't stop wanting your hands on my body—"

"Ally. Knock it off."

"—and your tongue in my mouth and my hands in your hair."

"Fuck. I don't want to hear this," he barks, running his own hands over that same hair as though he wants to pull it out by the roots. "I don't want it in my head."

He uses two fingers to jab his temple for emphasis. There's a spark of something in his expression that I haven't seen before. Something feverishly bright and maybe a little wild.

"I don't want to say it!" I can't keep a semi-hysterical laugh inside my mouth, much as I want to. I seem determined to make this entire conversation as humiliating for myself as possible. "But it's been a year. I remember everything you've ever said to me. Every look you've had on your face. Every time you've smiled, even if you never smile at me. I know it makes me pathetic, but I don't care. I'm past caring. I know you'd never cheat on your wife. I wouldn't want you to. And I promise I'll never mention this again. But I need to know. Please just tell me it's not all in my imagination. Do you ever think about me?"

I wait, my poor, silly heart in my throat, while it takes forever for him to school his features and wipe away the last remnants of whatever it was that I just saw. He seems flat as he shrugs. As devoid of human warmth as a marble bust in the nearest art museum. And his voice, when he speaks again, carries the awful finality of a crypt door clanging shut at the conclusion of a funeral service.

"I'm surprised at you, Harlow. You're better than this. Where's your pride?"

"I don't have any. Clearly," I say, hastily wiping away a tear the second it falls.

"Here's a tip: don't be a fool. Don't throw yourself at a man who will never feel the same way." His jaw tightens. For one second he looks as though his words cause him the same amount of pain that they cause me. But I know that it's my imagination. It always is when it comes to him. "Find the right guy. That's never going to be me."

I slowly come out of my memory trance, my cake plate empty and my cheeks wet with tears.

Find the right guy. That's never going to be me.

I reach for the remnants of the warm champagne and refill my glass, wishing I'd listened when he warned me way back then. I could have saved myself a fuck-load of heartache.

"GILDA, RIGHT?" I say to the owner of Valentina's European Bakery midmorning the next day, when I arrive to meet my sister for sorely needed crisis talks before I manage to blow my life up any further. Luckily, the place is mostly empty, which will allow for some privacy. I approach the counter, where dozens of beautiful and unidentifiable pastries sit inside their display case, waiting to spread sugar and calories throughout Greenwich Village. I can't help but think of Ally and what she'd say about all these treats amid her ongoing efforts to lose a little weight and smile inwardly. A feeling that's quickly followed by a throb of loss so acute it's a wonder I don't drop to my knees. "Good to see you again."

"I know you." Gilda puts down her cleaning spray and grins at me with the kind of delight you'd expect if you gave away stacks of Benjamins every time you showed up. She's wearing her pink uniform, which sparkles with all sorts of beads and whatnot, and she's got the matching twinkle in her eyes. I get the feeling that if she were, say, twenty years younger, she'd try to give Ally some competition for my masculine attention. "You're Mia's handsome devil of a brother. Why such a stranger? You haven't been back since we finished remodeling."

"Looks great," I say, taking a moment away from my abject misery to notice that the plastic sheeting is now gone and to appreciate the expanded dining area and what looks like a bigger kitchen on the other side of the counter. "I'm sure business is booming."

"It is," she says with unmistakable pride. "And you know that my niece Ella—not sure if you know Ella—has expanded into wedding cakes now. So that keeps her busy."

She points to several new oversized pictures on the wall that feature some amazing wedding cakes. The types of creations that I'm sure the society folks on the Upper East Side are happy to pay a couple of extra zeros for.

"Nice," I say.

"So..." She squints, pointing her finger at my face. "Black coffee and a Belgian waffle. Plain. Am I right? I never forget a face or an order."

"I'm impressed. And my sister's coming, too, but I have no idea what she'll want."

"*Men,*" she says, rolling her eyes and working on the coffee. "Mia always gets the Portuguese egg tarts and coffee with plenty of cream and sugar. You'd think her twin brother would know that."

"You'd think," I say, chuckling as I head for a table near the window overlooking the sidewalk. "I'll be over here. Thanks."

"My pleasure," she says, heading into the back.

I have a seat and do what I've been doing since I left

Ally's last night—namely, try to figure out how I single-handedly managed to plunge my great life into this cesspool of despair. I'm staring glumly at the passersby outside, wondering how they can look so happy when my life is now complete shit, when my sister hurries into view, sees me and waves.

I perk up because she's got a level head on her shoulders and is usually great with advice. Until Liam appears behind her, looking as thrilled to be part of the proceedings as I am to see him.

"Liam," she says happily as she sweeps inside.

"What the fuck is *he* doing here? I just saw him last night for drinks," I say, standing to give my sister a hug once they walk over. "I said I needed to talk, Mia. No offense," I add, now hugging Liam.

"None taken," he says, dropping into his seat with the resigned air of a man getting his bib pinned on for his annual dental cleaning. "This is not my idea of a good time. I'm only here because you helped me out the night we got engaged."

"This is an emergency, Liam," Mia says, sitting next to him. "It's an all-hands-on-deck situation. Why wouldn't you come?"

"Because I have a job. And a life," he says before glancing up as Gilda returns with a tray and shooting her a smile.

"Hi, Aunt Gilda," Mia says, propping up to give her a kiss on the cheek as Gilda unloads the coffee and pastries. "How are you?"

"If it isn't the lovebirds," Gilda says, now accepting a kiss from Liam.

"How are you?" Liam asks as she finishes with the tray.

"Very well indeed," Gilda says, blushing furiously. "And what can I get *you*?"

Liam glances over at the display case. "Coffee. Cream. What about a Napoleon? Do you serve Napoleons?"

"I've got you covered," she says, winking as she hurries off again.

"This is nice and all," I say before taking a fortifying sip of coffee. "But I don't know why we're *here*. I need a scotch and soda or ten. Especially with Liam here. Not a freaking *waffle*."

"I told you. This is the only time we were all available," Mia says before taking a hearty bite of her little pastry, generating a shower of flakes on her plate. "So what happened?"

I eyeball Liam warily.

"She'll tell me everything later anyway," he says, shrugging.

"Remind me to have a discussion with you later about privacy," I say, scowling at my sister.

"Yes, yes. Duly noted," she says, rolling her eyes as she gives me one of those *speed it up* gestures.

"So… It was her birthday yesterday—" I start.

"Oh my God," she says, exchanging a startled look with Liam. "Why does everything happen on birthdays? Why can't anyone have a normal birthday around here?"

That's right. I forgot that Mia's relationship with Liam came to a head *on our birthday* a couple of months ago. I won't get into it now, but it's a whole story about how I helped the two of them reconcile and get engaged. I suppose it was my fairy godfather moment.

"This isn't about *you*," I tell her. "This is about me torching my life."

"Well, what happened?" she asks. "You didn't forget, did you?"

"No," I say, reaching into my pocket, retrieving the jewelry box and slamming it onto the table. "And that reminds me. I never even got around to giving her *these*."

She lunges for the box and gets it open with a speed that suggests she's trying to qualify for some Olympic event. Then she gasps when she sees the pair of glittering diamond studs.

"Very nice," she says, eyeing me with a new appreciation. "I repeat: what happened?"

I try to get my thoughts together, but I find it difficult to explain how things unfolded last night. Even to myself.

"I went over there after we finished up with drinks last night," I tell Liam, who nods encouragingly. "She wasn't expecting me. She thought I didn't know it was her birthday. I gave her some flowers. She got really excited and she, ah, told me she loves me. For the first time."

Mia breaks into an ecstatic grin. "That's awesome," she says as Liam gives me a thumbs-up. "I'm so happy for you."

"Not so fast," I say. "I, ah, froze."

Rarely have I seen a smile disappear so quickly.

"You froze?" she says, a cold front sweeping across her face. "What do you mean, you *froze*?"

"Here we are," Gilda says just then, giving me a welcome reprieve as she arrives at the table with Liam's stuff. "Am I forgetting anything? Everything look okay? Let me know if you need anything else."

"Will do," Liam tells her. "Thanks."

Aunt Gilda smiles and retreats, leaving me to get

frostbite from the frigidity of Mia's glare. But before I can say anything, Liam starts, pulls his phone out of his breast pocket and checks the display.

"Whoops," he says, getting up and giving my sister a peck on the cheek. A gesture she doesn't bother to acknowledge because she's too busy using her flashing eyes to shoot laser strikes directly through my forehead. "Sorry. I need to take this. I'm consulting on a case. Be right back."

He walks off and goes outside to take the call and pace in front of our window.

"Well?" Mia demands.

"I don't know," I say, struggling to understand what happened to me in what should have been the best moment of my life.

I remember the glow in Ally's luminous eyes as she told me how she feels. Her unmistakable happiness. My responsive disbelief and the way it yielded to an explosion of joy. Then, without warning, the sudden flattening descent of paralysis. Like a trick stone wall dropping on Harrison Ford in an Indiana Jones movie. Worst of all, the way the light went out of her eyes and the knowledge that I killed it.

And for what?

Why did I do that? What happened to me? Before everything went sideways, I felt the happiest and luckiest I've ever felt in my life. The sensation was nothing like it was with my ex, even when our relationship was at its most harmonious. This thing with Ally? It's so much bigger than that. The two of us have so many more layers of peace, understanding and *fun*. I trust her. I depend on her. I need her. I crave her. Nothing she's ever done has given me the slightest hint of meaningful trouble on our horizon. I've never doubted her. Never feared she'd let me down in any significant way.

So *why*, in that beautiful moment that was the answer to every Ally-centered prayer I've had since the minute I met her, when she looked at me as though I'm the king of this universe and all universes yet to be discovered, did I take the emotional equivalent of a rocket-propelled grenade and blow the whole thing to smithereens?

"I froze up," I say with my ongoing incredulity. "I *screwed* up. She was honest. She put it all out there. She loves me. She wants us to move in together. She wants kids. A life. With *me*. She knows that already. Zero doubts."

"And naturally, since you're a man, you freaked out and ran screaming from the premises like your hair was on fire," Mia says acidly.

"No," I say, still struggling to process the way my emotions shut down on me and discover a way to convey it to her so she can give me the help I clearly need. I feel like Michelangelo chipping away at his block of marble and trying to find David inside even though there's no sign of him yet. "I just…couldn't believe it. It can't be real."

"Why not?" she asks, the glare giving way to a thoughtful frown.

"Because. My marriage was bad. Almost from the start. We worked on it, but it never got much better. I haven't been divorced that long. I wanted to connect with Ally, yeah, but I never got much further than that. I just figured that we'd, I don't know, enjoy each other for a while and see what happened. I didn't picture *this*."

"This *what*?"

"It's so easy with Ally," I say with a surge of

relief, as though I've chipped away a large chunk of marble and now have a better view of my thoughts. "Everything about being with her is easy. And *fun*. There's no drama. No misunderstandings. No awkward silences. No passive-aggressive behavior. On either end. It just...*works*. I didn't expect to come out of my divorce and find my life partner ten minutes later. I wasn't expecting her to be so open about her feelings so soon. I just... I don't know. I feel like this can't be right. I don't get to go from the saddest, loneliest, emptiest marriage in the world to paradise every day with Ally. There's gotta be a catch somewhere. A booby trap. Something I'm missing. Something I'm going to screw up. I'm not just suddenly going to succeed beyond my wildest dreams at this relationship when I fucked the other one up so badly."

Her expression clears. "Yes, you are, you unmitigated idiot," she says without missing a beat. "Because *Ally* is the right person for you and your ex wasn't. Hence, things work with Ally."

I stiffen, my brain clearing of everything except the knowledge that my sister has just dropped a profound truth directly on top of my thick head. The sensation is so overwhelming that it creates absolute and undeniable clarity.

Ally and I belong together. No one else could—or would—ever work. For either of us.

Duh.

It occurs to me that maybe I'm torturing myself for no good reason.

It occurs to me that maybe I could—and should —stop.

My fear packs its bags and takes off. Just like that. Gone.

I start to laugh, then catch myself as she continues speaking. I don't want to miss any of these sprinkled pearls of wisdom.

"You know what your problem is?" she continues. "You freaked yourself out because the only thing you've ever failed at in your whole life was the biggest thing. Your marriage."

"What?"

"You said so yourself. That you picked the wrong woman. You failed at picking the right woman. So now, here comes Ally and you don't trust your judgment. You figure if things aren't hard, they can't be right. The thing you don't understand is that things with Ally are easy *because* they're right. See how that works?"

"Yeah, okay, I get it," I say, starting to feel sheepish about the whole thing. What kind of idiot pushes away the love of his life when she throws herself at his feet? And to think I'm considered the best and the brightest of my generation. I've got a medical degree from a fancy private university, for fuck's sake. I guess it goes to show that book smarts don't translate to emotional intelligence or self-awareness. I'm just grateful that Liam wasn't here to witness my breakthrough moment. He would've laughed his ass off. "You don't have to be so smug. Don't act like *you've* had your shit together this whole time."

"Not at all," she says serenely. "The important thing to remember is that I got my shit together *before you did.*"

"Fair point," I say, laughing.

"So you love her? You want to marry her?" she asks eagerly. "I'm ready for a super-cool sister-in-law. God knows I suffered enough with the snotty last one."

We all did. "I'll get back to you on that," I say. Not because I don't know. But because it seems inappropriate to share that kind of information with Mia before I've told Ally herself.

"*What?* You can't clam up on me now. You can't leave me hanging!"

"I absolutely can," I say, digging into my waffle with gusto. All this emotional turmoil works up an appetite.

"Listen," Liam says, hurrying back inside and probably sparing me from being murdered in broad daylight by my sister. He zeros in on me as he puts his phone back into his pocket and resumes his seat. "Don't shoot yourself in the foot. You either love her, or you don't. You know which one it is. If you love her, go get her. And stop bothering us with your bullshit. We're busy people. We don't want to be bothered running down to Greenwich Village to help you out all the time. Especially when we also have to talk Jake down from the ledge his sexy nanny's got him on. I've only got so much energy for you two clowns. Okay? Okay."

He tears into his Napoleon, leaving my sister and I to burst into laughter as we fist-bump each other across the table.

I ENDURE an exhausting day at the hospital. I'm not sure which one keeps me busier—trying not to cry or trying to avoid Michael. The emotional strain on top of the complete lack of sleep last night makes me cranky. So I hurry home at the earliest opportunity, shower and throw on my cute summer jammies. I'm determined to unwind while huddled on the sofa watching the latest true crime documentary and eating pizza and leftover birthday cake.

I've just arranged my blanket and reached for the remote when someone knocks at the door.

I freeze and stifle a curse. Only one person ever knocks like that. So much for telling the doorman not to automatically let Michael up anymore.

I stay right where I am, thinking hard. I could wait him out and pretend I'm not here, but then I wouldn't get to watch anything because he'd hear the TV. Plus, I have no idea how long he'd stick around if he's got a bee in his bonnet about speaking with me—which he apparently *does*—and I can't very well pretend not to be home when the pizza arrives. I'm not ready to speak with Michael and hear his lame excuses for not feeling the same way about me that I feel about him, but I'm unwilling to sacrifice my dinner to cowardice. I guess I could —

"I know you're in there, Ally," comes his voice through the door. "I can hear you avoiding me."

I throw off the blanket and head for the door, furious that I'm trapped and therefore forced to deal with him at my own damn apartment, which should be a safe zone. Especially after I put so much effort into avoiding him earlier and barely emerged with my sanity intact. I deserve some relaxation. I deserve ten lousy seconds without thoughts of him eating away at every corner of my brain.

"What are you even doing up here?" I call. "I told the doorman not to let you up anymore."

"He mentioned that. But when I gave him a large tip to thank him for taking such good care of you, he seemed to change his mind about the whole thing."

"Oh my *God*," I say, smacking my forehead and pacing in front of the door. Now, on top of everything else, I need to deal with a disloyal doorman. This is all hitting way too close to home. "What do you want, Dr. Jamison?"

"*Dr. Jamison*. That's a step in the wrong direction," he mutters. "I want to talk to you. We could have done it at the hospital if you hadn't been avoiding me all day. Now I have to stoop to skulking around in hallways and bribing doormen."

"Seems like you would've connected the dots and figured out that I was avoiding you because I don't want to talk to you. Because there's nothing left to say. We were both crystal clear on our positions last night."

"Untrue. *You* were clear. *I* was unprepared."

Like that makes it any better. If someone gives you a winning lotto ticket, you don't tell them to come back tomorrow because you were unprepared to receive visitors today.

"Unprepared for *what*?" I say, sweeping my arms wide as I face the door. "If you considered me being in love with you a good thing, it seems like you would've quickly become prepared."

There's a long pause. So long that I get the awful sensation that he's walked away. And I can't begin to convey the sickening feeling of disappointment at the idea that he has.

"Are you there?" I snap.

"Yeah," he says, sounding gruff now. "To answer your question, I was unprepared to get everything I want in life so quickly and so easily."

Wait, *what*?

My heart screeches to a complete stop.

I open my mouth but quickly discover that *I'm* now the one who can't make their words work.

"Ally?" He sounds closer now.

I step closer to the door. "Yeah," I manage faintly, my mouth drying out. "I'm here."

"I'd like a do-over on your birthday. Please."

"A do-over?"

"Yeah. Can we do that?"

"I don't know," I say, now eager to hear what he has to say and equally eager not to climb back on an emotional roller coaster. I just don't have the energy for it. Not tonight.

"I won't blame you if you say no, but…I guarantee you'll like this birthday better."

"I don't—"

"*Ally*. Trust me. Let's take it from the top."

Like the ending was ever in any question. That's my biggest problem with Michael.

He gets me every time.

"Fine," I say, reaching for the lock. But he knocks again, surprising me.

I hesitate before deciding to play along.

"Ah...who is it?" I call.

"It's me," he says, his voice sounding much cheerier now.

I think hard, trying to remember everything I said last night. "What're you doing here? I thought you were having drinks with your friends."

"You skipped that whole part about having a mask on your face," he reminds me. "But it's fine. I'll improvise. You're the one who should be scared. Why did I have to find out from HR that it's your birthday?"

"Sorry," I say, laughing as I swing the door open. "I wasn't sure what I should do— *Oh, they're gorgeous!*"

He's got another massive bouquet slung over his arm, long-stemmed pink tulips with greenery this time. But I'm much more interested in him. His eyes are warm, his cheeks dimpled. There's an air of expectancy about him that makes him seem, I don't know, almost buoyant. As though he can barely contain himself. Seeing him like this creates the sweetest ache of yearning inside me that it breaks my heart in the best possible way. If there is such a thing.

Even so, he hurt me last night. My tender feelings are still a little sore.

"Thank you," I say, stepping back to let him inside, my cheeks in flames. "I really appreciate your thoughtfulness. Would you like a slice of leftover birthday cake?"

His dimples deepen with a good-humored smile. "I don't think that's what you said last night," he says quietly as he comes in and shuts the door before setting the flowers on the nearest chair. "I think you're skipping something."

I make a show of scrunching up my face and tapping my chin with my forefinger. "There was a whole thing about Friday the thirteenth," I say.

"That's not the part I was thinking about."

We stare at each other while I try to regulate the input and output from my lungs. But it's not easy to do with my heart pounding out a thousand beats per minute.

"I'm so scared right now," I shakily admit.

"Don't be."

His gaze is steady. So warm. There's no way I can hold anything back.

"I love you," I say, my voice little more than a whisper.

"I love you too."

He says it on a burst of breathless emotion that twists up his expression as he reaches out to take my face in his hands. He presses fevered kisses to my hair and my forehead. My eyes, both cheeks and finally, sweetly, my lips. "I love you so fucking much, Ally. It's the biggest thing in my life."

I laugh and hug him close with profound gratitude, dizzy with relief and determined to savor every second of this moment.

"That's the kind of birthday present I can get behind."

"I mean it," he says, pulling back and ducking his head just enough for his blue eyes to take up my entire field of vision. "There's nothing I wouldn't do for you. Or give you. It's my job now to take care of you and make sure you're happy. That's what makes *me* happy."

Overwhelmed with joy as I am right now, the Oprah-trained feminist in me insists on making a brief appearance.

"I'm a grown woman," I say, working hard to give him a stern look. "I'm responsible for myself."

"Of course," he says with equally fake gravity, one corner of his mouth twitching.

"That said, you just nailed my whole happiness thing. Well done."

We laugh together, quickly followed by another round of urgent kissing that ends when he tightens his hands on either side of my head and breaks away.

"I'm not done. You're moving in with me. Now. I don't care when your lease is up. And I don't know why I have to think of everything around here."

"But are you sure you have room?" I deadpan.

"We'll figure something out," he says, all boyish delight.

"Thank God. I was afraid I'd be homeless soon. Or worse, living on Kelly's sofa."

"Nope. I own your nights now. Oh, and I bought you a Range Rover," he says, snapping his fingers. "Almost forgot. They'll deliver it in the morning."

"A *Range Rover*?" I say, startled by the segue. "I wasn't aware I was in the market for a car. And I can buy my own car if I need one."

"Do you have any idea how much money I have now?" he says with a tinge of exasperation.

"Yeah, but—"

"But nothing. I don't like you driving around in that old Camry. You need something sturdier."

"Camrys are very safe," I say, part of me ready to square up if he's going to disparage my car while the other part of me wonders why the hell I'm arguing about such an amazing gift.

"Absolutely," he says, his skilled hands working their way under the edge of my pajama top and massaging the small of my back. "And your beloved Camry has earned its retirement with our thanks for keeping you safe this whole time."

"Anything else?" I ask warily, feeling my brows creep higher at the stunning pace of breaking events. I know I'm being handled, but I need to pick my fights right now. Especially when this new distraction is making my blood sizzle and therefore pushing the car situation to the bottom of my list of pressing issues.

"Yeah." A silky note enters his voice as he eases closer, angles his mouth within kissing range and uses his thumbs to trace lazy circles low on my sides. "I really want to fuck you."

We stare at each other, heat surging between us.

"That seems like a good idea," I say, rising on my tiptoes to meet him.

Everything changes the second his mouth covers mine. These are no longer smiling and happy kisses of relief. These are incendiary kisses designed to leave nothing behind but a pile of ashes and maybe a spark or two. He grabs fistfuls of my hair on either side and uses them to tilt my head way back for complete access. He takes my mouth hard, fucking me with his tongue and demanding surrender. I give it eagerly, moaning for him. Sucking him deeper. Nipping and biting.

He works his way lower, nuzzling my neck and leaving no nerve ending behind in his quest to make them all tingle. His hands glide across my bare skin and sweep my top over my head and off in one smooth movement. The two of us work on my shorts and panties together, easing them past my hips and down so I can kick them the rest of the way off. Then he palms my ass and exerts enough pressure to tell me what he wants. I hop up into his arms, wrapping my legs around his waist and my arms around his neck. He rubs his face against my jiggling breasts, breathing me in as we head for the sofa. His fingers never miss a trick and take advantage of my position to stroke the slick cleft between my thighs as I helplessly thrust against him.

I'm ready. I'm *so* ready.

I'm braced for him to lay me down on my back, but he has other plans, dropping into a seated position with me straddling him. I rise just enough to get my hands between us and undo his belt and pants. Then he quickly takes over, rumbling with rising impatience as he moves his boxers aside and grips himself.

I'm poised with my legs spread and ready to tell him to *hurry*, but something about the look on his face in this arrested moment stops me. He's so still and focused as he stares up at me, so openly adoring that his eyes seem to glow. I get the feeling that I'm seeing the real him for the first time. Or maybe I'm seeing *all* of him for the first time.

I start to smile.

He starts to smile.

No words required.

I slowly ease down onto him while simultaneously licking my way deep into his voluptuous mouth. We begin to surge together, our tempo languid. Why hurry when we have the rest of the night and, even better, the rest of our lives? I circle my hips, taking care to brush my nipples against his chest and grind my sweet spot against his groin as my hair swings on either side of his face. Ever helpful, he matches my rhythm as he kneads the two halves of my ass together, concentrating and intensifying my pleasure as it spirals lower.

Funny how people make fun of men for coming too fast. I'm lucky I last thirty seconds before the buildup of exquisite sensation crescendos and overflows. A single high note of astonishment and I'm done with a piercing orgasm that jackknifes through me before subsiding into aftershocks that go on and on.

He laughs, a darkly triumphant rumble that somehow increases *my* joy, before stiffening and surging against me a final time. Then he shouts my name in a voice that's hoarse and thrilling. We ride it out together, holding each other closer until there's nothing left but gasps for air, dissipating heat and unadulterated *joy*.

I collapse against him, my smiling lips pressed to the side of his neck as he slumps back against the cushions.

I'm happy to stay there until I die, or at least until looming starvation forces me to answer the door for the pizza guy when he gets here, but something hard is hurting the side of my knee. Something in his pocket.

I raise my head and frown.

"What's this?" I say with a nudge.

"What?" he says drowsily, cracking his eyes open and reaching into the pocket. "Oh, that? Another birthday present. I would have given it to you last night, but one of us flipped out."

"*I* didn't flip out."

"My memory is hazy."

"And how many presents do I get?" I ask, stunned by this ongoing generosity. "I'm not that special. And it's not even a big birthday."

"You're special enough," he says with a wry twist of his mouth as he hands me a flat red jeweler's box that comes from Cartier, unless I'm much mistaken. "It's not that big a deal. Just some diamond studs."

"Did you say *just* diamond studs?" I cry, my heart cartwheeling with excitement. "Oh my God. Thank you!"

"Don't thank me till you see them." He represses a grin with what looks like great difficulty. "You better check them out to see if you like them."

"*Like* them? Who the hell doesn't like diamond studs from —"

I stop dead as I open the box.

It's not a pair of diamond studs.

It's a pear-shaped diamond ring with baguettes on either side. The most gorgeous ring in the world. A dream engagement ring.

My heart sinks.

"Hope you kept the receipt," I say, trying to manage my disappointment. What a snafu. No diamond studs for me tonight. I snap the box shut and hand it to him before I get too attached to this ring and/or, worse, somehow damage it before he manages to return it to the store in exchange for my earrings. "They gave you the wrong box."

There's a pause.

"I don't think they did, Ally," he says quietly, staring me dead in the face.

Wow. Funny. He's got jokes. Just to add insult to injury.

"Take it," I say irritably, thrusting the box at him again.

A hint of a smile softens his eyes, making those sexy crow's-feet appear at the outer corners.

"Ally," he says with infinite tenderness. "I'm not taking the ring back. And I'm not asking you. I'm telling you. We're getting married."

Have you ever been struck by lightning? Right through the top of your head?

It's hard to get breath back after that. Impossible to think straight.

I blink. I gasp. I sputter something that has no words attached to it. I look down at the box in my hand, then back up at him.

"But—"

"Ally. We belong together. We've both always known that. We're getting married."

I search hard, looking for any detectable sign of uncertainty and finding only open adoration. As though this wonderful man loves me exactly as much as I love him.

"Oh my God," I say, lapsing into a hysterical hybrid of laughing and crying as I fling my arms around his neck and feel his tighten around my waist. "We're getting *married*."

"GREAT DRESS, BY THE WAY," Michael says, taking my hand as we head down the sidewalk. "That pale yellow is your color."

"You think so?" I say, using my free hand to straighten the belt's bow. It's hard to go wrong with a wrap dress. This one is simple, fluttery and elegant. Basically summer in a garment, plus it does wonders in terms of sprucing up my extra pounds. "It's amazing what getting out of your scrubs and throwing on some heels every now and then can do for a person. And with you complimenting me like that, I'm going to start to feel like a sexy woman."

"You *are* a sexy woman," he says, his appreciative gaze sweeping me up and down with a pointed detour around the cleavage area. "I plan to remind you later."

"My memory isn't what it used to be, but didn't you just remind me this morning?" I ask, a purr creeping into my voice.

"Do I hear a complaint?"

"The one thing you'll never hear from me in that department is a complaint," I assure him.

Those blue eyes of his smile at me over the top of my hand as he brings it to his mouth for a lingering kiss.

"Good."

"You look very sexy yourself in your gray suit," I say. "Your tie even matches my dress."

"Huh. Interesting."

"I'm still not sure what the occasion is," I say.

"I told you. Between work and all this crazy wedding planning, we need a special lunch. Something just for the two of us."

"Agreed. I'm not looking a gift horse in the mouth. At all. As long as we're done in time to get to Valentina's for the cake tasting at three. We wouldn't want to miss that."

"Fear not."

"Is our restaurant on the river? I was hoping we might get a glimpse of Lady Liberty. I don't think I've been this far south since the night of the dinner cruise for Dr. Smith. You probably don't remember that night."

"Funny. You came with another guy," he says with a narrowed sidelong glance. "I remember *that*."

"My point is," I continue loudly, "that it's hard to believe it's been a year. And that we'll be married in just a couple more months — *oh, look*. Speaking of weddings."

I point at the city clerk's building across the street, which is basically Manhattan's answer to Vegas' Little Wedding Chapel. A cottage quickie wedding industry has sprung up including photographers, flowers and even wedding rings. Everything one needs for the cere-mony seems to be available for purchase. Several happy couples, wearing everything from full-on cathedral-worthy gowns, veils and tuxedos down to matching track suits and sneakers, mill around, chattering happily.

"That's how to do it. Quick and easy," Michael says. "They all look like geniuses from where I'm standing."

"Yeah, me too," I say wistfully as we stop and watch them. "As we celebrate the first anniversary of our endless engagement."

"Don't get me started," he says, scowling.

I know what he means. Planning a wedding is not for the faint of heart. Especially in NYC, where venues tend to book up years in advance.

I open my mouth, struggling to put my ambivalence into words. I'm getting my dream wedding with my dream man. Nothing to complain about here, folks.

And yet...

"I still want the big wedding with all our friends," I say.

"And your custom dress from Mia. Don't forget *that*," he says with a wry smile.

"And my custom dress from Mia. I want *that* for sure." The thought of my gorgeous dress makes me grin. On the other hand, the reminder of all the waiting we've done in our relationship makes me sigh. "But I wish we were already married."

"I was hoping you'd say that," he says with grim satisfaction as he tightens his grip on my hand. "Let's go."

And he takes off for the crosswalk, tugging me along with him.

"Go?" I say with an incredulous laugh. "Go *where*?"

"Let's go get married," he says without breaking stride.

"What, *now*?"

"Yes," he says with that quiet intensity that always makes my heart stop. *"Now."*

I stop dead and glance wildly around, wondering if I'm being pranked. This is all too good to be true.

"We can't just get married!"

"Sure we can," he says.

"We don't have an appointment."

"Don't need one."

"Michael," I say, determined to talk some sense into him. "We don't have our marriage license with us."

Without a word, he reaches into his breast pocket and produces...A white envelope that looks suspiciously like our marriage license.

Oh, my God.

"We don't have our rings," I say, now feeling equal swoops of excitement and hope.

Could we really get married? Today? Right now?

One of those dark brows shoots up as he reaches into the pocket of his slacks and produces...The black velvet box that contains our wedding bands.

"What about flowers? A photographer?" My voice pitches higher. "I refuse to get married without pictures."

He flashes a smug smile as he raises a hand and gestures at someone. I follow his line of sight and watch as a photographer and a woman with a bouquet of flowers detach from the crowd and head in our direction. The bouquet, I note with astonishment, is full of flowers in delicate yellow and cream colors.

The perfect complement to my dress.

"I'm beginning to think I've been lied to," I say, rounding on him. My voice is now tinged with creeping hysteria, which is what emotional ecstasy will do for you. I can't believe that I'm finally going to become his wife.

Just like that. Well…Five years and *then*, suddenly, just like that. "I'm beginning to think this outing isn't about a special lunch at a Thai restaurant at all. You were probably going to wear a *blue* tie today. I'm beginning to think you engineered this whole thing."

My consternation seems to amuse him.

"And if I did?"

"What about our big wedding? What about all our planning?"

"I have *one* plan. To marry you," he says quietly. "I'm happy to do it twice. As long as we do it today."

The tenderness in his tone undoes me. Completely. I have no words and an abundance of happy tears as I wrap my arms around his neck and pull him in for several dozen fervent kisses.

He cups my head in his hands, his urgency matching mine until we're both breathless and maybe a little misty. Then he pulls back, resting his forehead against mine

"I love you so much," I say.

"I love you."

I try to let it go at that, but I can't stop a helpless confession.

"I get so scared sometimes," I whisper.

"Of what, Angel? Why be scared on our wedding day?"

"Of you not loving me as much as I love you."

"Not possible," he says with a shaky laugh.

"Sometimes I think about all the things that had to line up for us to be together like this. All the things that had to change. What if it hadn't worked out for us?"

"Also not possible. You know why?"

"No," I say, mesmerized by the huskiness in his tone and the way the early afternoon sun hits his eyes just right, making them sparkle like a handful of flawless aquamarines.

"Because you're the other half of my heart. I knew that on some level the day I met you. I pretended I didn't know that but I'm a surgeon. And *you're* a surgeon. Surgeons know that no one can live with half their heart missing. Can they?"

I hastily wipe away a tear and lean in for another kiss.

"No," I say. "They cannot."

"I came back to be with you. As soon as I could."

"Took you too damn long," I grumble.

Once corner of his mouth twitches with a repressed smile.

"Sorry about that."

"Luckily for you, I'm in a forgiving mood today."

"Good." He pulls back, his dimples deepening as he takes my hand again. "Can we get married? Now that we're on the same page?"

"Absolutely," I say happily, falling into step beside him as we head to the crosswalk. "But I still want my special lunch. I was promised Thai food."

"Anything for you," he says, laughing as he wraps his arm around me and leads me into the clerk's office — and my life as his wife.

Keep reading for an excerpt from Liam & Mia's story (where Michael makes his first appearance, BTW), ***His Lost Love***!

EXCERPT FROM HIS LOST LOVE

Chapter 1 — Liam

"Liam." Michael Jamison, one of my closest buddies since we met at freshman orientation at NYU fourteen years ago, blocks the door, preventing me from entering his new apartment in downtown Manhattan. His scowl suggests that I've come strapped with explosives and begun waving the detonation button in his face. "What the hell are you doing here?"

I shrug and try to look harmless as I pass him the nice bottle of wine I brought as a gift.

"Unless I'm mistaken, you're throwing your little housewarming tonight."

I gesture over his shoulder, where a sizable crowd has assembled and appears to be happily enjoying cocktails and jazzy music against the panoramic backdrop of the Hudson River with the Jersey skyline in the distance. He and another college friend of ours, Jake Quinn, recently went public with the medical device company I started a few years back. I should mention that I got a degree in chemical and biomedical engineering before I went to Harvard Med and became a cardiac surgeon. Hey. I'm brilliant, ambitious and talented. Don't expect me to apologize for it. Anyway, I won't bore you with the details, but I invented a couple of devices that make cardiac procedures a hell of a lot easier. Michael and Jake were my early investors. I combined money I inherited on my father's death together with their money. Which means that we've all experienced a significant uptick in our bottom line this year, although I still practice because that's my first love. Now we all try to out-apartment and out-car each other. And I plan to start dabbling more in the real estate market when a good opportunity presents itself.

"I thought I'd check the place out," I continue. "You know I'm interested in real estate."

"Cut the bullshit," he says, his scowl deepening as he snatches the bottle. "You're here because you want to see my sister."

I arrange my expression into something that hopefully suggests that the idea never crossed my mind.

"I just want to catch the view you've been bragging about." I crane my neck, trying to see past his big head, but there's no sign of her. Mia, his twin, was also in our class at NYU, by the way. "Looks nice. Your apartment could almost be a boat that sits directly on the water. Not as nice as *my* view, though. You letting me in?"

"No. I've been walking a tightrope ever since the two of you imploded back when we graduated. You think it's easy for me to be Switzerland all the time when the two of you have avoided each other for years? Now she's going to think that I set this whole thing up so you could ambush her."

"Yeah, well, now I'm back in town." I moved back last year during my mother's final illness. Now that I've settled her estate, it's time for me to settle things with Mia. "It's past time for Mia and me to stop avoiding each other. We're fully grown adults now. Not hotheaded kids. The city should be big enough for both of us."

"Couldn't agree more. Why don't you text her and see if she wants to grab coffee or drinks like a normal person?"

"Because I'm here now." The part I don't mention? That I've worked up the courage to show up tonight and doubt I'll be able to produce any new courage if I leave without seeing her and then need to text her. I decide to drop the act. "Is she here?"

"She's here," he says grimly.

I feel a tremendous surge of adrenaline. And something that feels strangely like triumph.

"What's it going to be?" I ask.

"Fine." He jerks the door all the way open and lets me pass. "Just make sure she knows that this was *your* idea. I didn't want you here, and you know it."

"That's not strictly true," I say, now scanning the room for any sign of her. "You said you were having your housewarming tonight. You also said that Mia would be here. I took that as a warm invitation to enjoy your hospitality."

"Huh. Funny. Because I'm positive I stated it as a dire warning for you to stay away."

"Semantics," I say, then catch sight of Jake, who materializes out of the crowd with a scotch and soda for my benefit. I receive it with a grateful one-handed hug and a pointed look in Michael's direction. "Finally. A *true* friend."

"Fuck you," Michael says mildly.

"Saw you coming," Jake tells me as I take an appreciative sip to shore up my nerves. "What'd I miss?"

"Liam's here to see Mia," Michael supplies with his usual stir-the-pot enthusiasm and wicked glee at someone else's discomfort.

"Fuck *you*," I tell him, then spy her across the room and experience a sudden catastrophic system failure that freezes me to the spot. Seriously. It's a wonder I don't choke on my tongue.

These two, naturally, notice immediately.

"You planning to grow a pair and talk to her?" Jake asks me, not bothering to hide his sudden obnoxious smirk. "Or are you going to stand here picking your nose all night?"

"I'm betting on the latter," Michael says. "Knowing Liam like I do. Based on long and painful history. Speaking of history, what was that Julius Caesar quote? We talked about it in ancient history freshman year."

"What, *I came, I saw, I conquered*?" Jake says.

"That's the one." Michael claps me on the back with his free hand and gives my shoulders a squeeze that makes me want to see how many of his gleaming teeth I can knock out with a single punch. "I'm thinking Liam's quote would be *I came, I saw, I froze*."

"Either that or *I came, I saw, I shat the bed*."

With that, my two so-called best friends launch into a round of raucous laughter at my expense. Not that I don't deserve it at this point in the evening, when my ongoing paralysis acts as an embarrassment to me and probably my entire family for two or three generations back. Still, I wonder what it is about these two idiots that has made me keep them around this whole time. Probably the threat of blackmail for all the dumb shit they witnessed me do.

I unstick myself with tremendous effort and peel my eyes away from her long enough to glare at these two. Mia Jamison and I are ancient history. This doesn't have to be a whole big thing. There's no reason why the two of us can't exchange a quick greeting and break the ice after all this time. Clarification: no reason except that a) she's so engrossed in a conversation with some woman that she doesn't know I'm here yet; and b) I'm still trying to grow that pair of balls I'll need to make the long walk across the room to say hello to her.

"Maybe if I had better wingmen, I'd be over there by now," I say bitterly, gesturing to a passing server for a refill on my scotch and soda. "How about you help a guy out rather than kicking him when he's down?"

"Look," Michael says, his amusement vanishing. He slings that arm around my shoulder again, reeling me in for a few urgent words of advice. "You're building this up in your mind. She's still just Mia. The same girl you met on our study abroad in Rome."

That's exactly what I'm afraid of.

Luckily, the server returns with my drink just then. I snatch it off his tray, and down the entire thing in a couple of rough gulps.

"*Go.*" Michael relieves me of my empty glass and jerks his head in her direction. "Say hi. Get it over with. It's getting harder the longer you stand here. You're thirty-four fucking years old. You know how to talk to a woman."

That's true. But there are standard human women. And then there's Mia Jamison.

Separate categories.

"You're right," I say grimly, more because I'm sick of myself than from any sudden infusion of courage. "I need you two to keep eyes on the situation for me. Be on standby. Keep the car running. Maybe get a fire extinguisher. Just in case."

We all laugh.

"Get outta here," Jake says. "Report back."

"You got it."

"And if you hurt my sister again? I'll kill you," Michael adds with a hard glint of bloody murder in his eyes.

I take off without disputing his assertion about who did the hurting in my relationship with Mia. My feet get heavier as I work my way through the crowd, which is elegant and nicely liquored by now. By the time I get within ten feet of her, they weigh a ton apiece. My steps slow. My heart races. And all I can do is stare, because there she is after all this time and I can't fucking believe it.

Mia Nova Jamison.

My first love. The woman whose image, smile and laugh burrowed their way into my brain one Roman summer when I was twenty and have remained there ever since. Resisting all my best efforts to eradicate them.

Like malaria or the kudzu that suffocates trees in the South.

I'm not happy about my excitement here, mind you. Why? Because I hate Mia Jamison for the way she left my life and for the condition she left me in when she did it. I should mention that up front. And I'm not talking about your garden-variety hate, as in *I hate sushi. Let's get pizza instead*. I'm talking about the kind of hate that gets stronger over time, rotting you from the inside out.

Sometimes it simmers. Sometimes it boils. Either way, the hate has no problem whatsoever existing alongside my ongoing fascination with this one woman.

Even so, my lingering hard feelings don't stop me from staring at her. And I doubt they'll ever stop me from wanting her.

You can't blame me for that. She's got a Liv Tyler vibe that's enough to make people lightheaded when they see her. But her hair is blacker, her skin paler and her eyes bluer. Her dimpled smile is all her own, as radiant as a Tahitian sunrise. She's always been lean and athletic. That hasn't changed if the way her strappy and slinky black dress pours over her thighs is any indication. With a dress like that, you start to wonder about the panty situation. If any. She wears a pair of killer heels that really work for her, but not as well as they work for me and my impressionable dick.

She laughs at something the woman says. The husky sound combines with the flash of her white teeth and the confident way she flips her hair over her bare shoulder to form something glorious. I can't lie about it. She's on top of the world tonight, clearly. I allow myself to be mesmerized and wallow in that smile for several suspended seconds.

I'm allowed. I haven't seen it for twelve years.

But then, without warning, she turns her head in my direction as though she's heard my heart thundering over all the ambient noise. No surprise there. The two of us were always great at creating our own energy field. Our gazes connect across the ten feet that separate us. I feel that connection as a zap of electricity shoots straight up my spine. She stiffens, her eyes widening. Her smile fades, leaving something stricken behind as color floods her face. She recovers quickly, peeling her attention away from me and recapturing most of her social graces for the benefit of her friend, but she's not that good an actress.

Except for the part when she acted like she gave a rat's ass about me back when we were in college.

That was good.

This? The unmistakable flare of panic in her big baby blues? The glitch in her composure as she smooths her hair with a hand that now looks a little shaky? She's rattled and she can't hide it. I consider that a win. God knows she's done nothing but rattle me since the day I laid eyes on her.

In a stroke of good luck, I complete my approach just as the woman excuses herself from Mia, leaving Mia to hesitate before squaring her shoulders and turning to face me. Maybe she was tempted to take off with the woman, but the Mia I thought I knew would never do that. She's many things—merciless witch comes to mind —but a coward isn't one of them.

Sure enough, she hitches up her chin, eyes glittering.

"Liam Wilder. I wasn't expecting to see you here."

I shrug and slide my hands in my pockets, buying myself time to get my shit together. It's not easy to think straight while being in her presence and hearing the throaty sound of her voice again.

"I'm full of surprises."

"That you are. I didn't know that Michael had invited you."

"He didn't, but I'm sure that was an oversight." I ease closer, arrested by the subtle defiance in her expression and by her scent, some carnal blend of flowers that defies description and is exactly the way I remember it. "You probably didn't know I was back in town."

"Odd, huh? You'd think a news flash like that would make the front page of the *Times*."

I laugh. I can't help it. One of the most intriguing things about Mia has always been the way she sharpens her tongue and wields it like a samurai sword, slicing and dicing people like a professional.

"Actually, Michael did mention you were back in the city." She hesitates. "And that your mother had died. Sorry to hear that. I'm sure it wasn't easy."

"Thanks," I say, which is all I can manage when I think about my mother's decline and death. She wasn't a gem in the mother department, but she was the only parent I had left, given my father's sudden cardiac arrest death right before I started college. Not to mention the fact that Mia seems concerned for me, and a tender emotion from Mia is, sadly, like a hit of heroin to a recovering addict.

I am evidently the addict in question. No recovery here, boy.

"Did dying make her any nicer?"

"Nope," I say with a startled laugh. "It'll take more than a visit from the Grim Reaper to soften my mother up."

She starts to smile with me, then catches herself and stops.

"You look great, by the way," I blurt.

One of those delicate brows goes up.

"I pay a personal trainer, a hairstylist and an aesthetician to keep me spackled together these days. Glad to know I'm not wasting my money. And you're not trying to flirt with me, are you?"

"Would it work?"

"Absolutely. Just like me going outside right now and trying to swim across the river to Jersey would work."

I laugh again, somehow resisting the growing urge to swallow her whole. She's *that* delicious.

"You looked great before all that, as I recall. Matter of fact, back in the day, I'd be looking forward to the end of the night and figuring out what you've got on under that dress." I pause to give her a once-over that lingers on her small breasts, curious to see if the attention is enough to make her nipples bead the way they used to. Ah. There it is. So that hasn't changed. Thrilling. "And you'd be looking forward to letting me."

Those luscious lips curl into a crooked smile without a trace of humor in it.

"Twenty-year-olds aren't known for their smarts. Back in the day, I survived on frozen pizza, donuts, diet soda and five hours of sleep most nights."

"Don't expect me to apologize for the sleep deprivation," I say, sweet memories making my voice husky. "We had better things to do in bed, as I vividly recall."

The bright patches of color in her cheeks intensify.

"Maybe, but I'm trying to stay away from stupid now that I'm older. If there's nothing else? I want to mingle with the people I actually want to see. Have a great night."

She turns to go, but I'm not done here. Not by a long shot. Not when being in Mia's presence again makes me feel this buzzed and *alive*. I don't know what I've been doing with my life this whole time, but it wasn't *this*. And *this* is something I need a lot more of.

"I understand you're designing for one of the big houses these days," I say quickly, before she can take off.

I try to recall which one it was, but my overstimulated brain can't call up the information at the moment. Ralph Lauren, maybe. "I'm impressed."

She makes a derisive sound. "Sure you are."

"I'm dead serious," I say, feeling a surge of the hate again, along with the sour taste of bile in the back of my mouth. "I know *exactly* how much your career in fashion means to you. Although I could have sworn you said you wanted to design wedding dresses. Or am I remembering that wrong?"

I realize my arrow hit home by the way she stiffens.

"Oh, so *that's* why you're here." She says it with the grim triumph of Sherlock Holmes when he slides that last clue into place and discovers who the murderer is. "Career advice."

Wrong. I want to remind her that I still exist. That while *she* may be living her Oprah-sanctioned best life, some of us aren't so lucky. That she still has her nasty claw marks all over my life.

"Well, that's why you ran off to Milan after graduation, right? To learn to make wedding dresses? So you could start your own atelier one day?"

"There was no *running away* involved," she says, the thinning of her lips belying her sweet tone and evident determination not to let me ruffle her feathers. "I got an apprenticeship in Milan and moved there."

"What about your dream of making wedding dresses?"

"Not all dreams go the distance," she says, her expression stony now. "But since you're so curious, you should know that I periodically make custom dresses for people through word of mouth. Matter of fact, I have a wedding this weekend."

I know that already, but now is not the time to mention it. Not when she's raised such an interesting topic.

"Any other dreams in particular?"

"Not at all," she says smoothly.

"Glad to hear it, Starlight," I say, adding a nice layer of mockery to my voice because I know it will infuriate her. And because I want to punish her for acting like the two of us didn't have joint dreams that died an ugly death. "I'm glad you have everything you ever wanted. And that there are no lingering hard feelings. No need for things to be awkward between old friends."

"We're not *old friends*." She can barely get the last two words out. For one thrilling second, I wonder if she actually wants to take a swing at me. I find my ongoing ability to push her buttons fascinating, I must say. "And don't call me *Starlight*."

"Why not? Nova is still your middle name, right? It means *star*, doesn't it?" I keep my voice silky. "Starlight is a perfectly good nickname even if you're not *my* star anymore. Why change things up at this late date? You're free to call me by *my* nickname if you want."

"*Asshole*? You don't mind me using that to your face?"

"No," I say with a startled laugh. "Brad Pitt."

"I'll pass on that. If there's nothing else…?"

She takes another step away, eager to leave me.

I hastily catch her warm arm and press my thumb to the thumping pulse in her wrist, twice as eager to keep her here. The reaction is instantaneous. Her eyes widen. Heat flares between us, exactly the way you get a whoosh of a flame when you light a gas grill.

"Are you here with someone?" I ask.

I hate myself for the sudden urgency in my voice,

which reveals my eternal weakness for her. But not as much as I hate her for bringing it out in me when I've done my best—for *years* I've done my best—to hide it if I can't overcome it.

"My personal life hasn't been any of your business for years, Liam," she says. "As you know."

She manages a lot of vehemence, but I'm fixated on the flickering heat between us. And the way she doesn't pull away. My gaze drops to her dewy lips. My mouth actually waters, which is what happens when you're dying for a taste of something.

I have a tough time hoisting my attention back to her glittering eyes, but I manage eventually.

"I'm not so sure about that. Have a drink with me. Let's see where the night takes us."

That does it.

"There's no *us*," she says, finally pulling free and using that same hand to give my cheek a sharp and condescending pat. "I know there's no other woman in the world like me, but I'm sure there are several here who'd be happy to hook up with you tonight if you twinkle those hazel eyes at them."

"What if I twinkle them at *you*? Will that work?"

Crooked smile from Mia. She takes a step back toward me. Eases closer. Tips her chin up as though she wants to kiss me. *I* ease closer and dip my head, planning to let her.

"Poor Liam. You need to understand that I would go back to my studio, find a needle and thread and sew my pussy shut before I *ever* gave you the pleasure again."

I bark out a laugh, riveted by this woman who surely knows that nothing makes my blood race like a challenge.

"We'll see about that. *Starlight.*"

She looks murderous as she pivots and stalks off in those killer heels, giving me the distinct pleasure of watching her hips and ass work in perfect synchronicity as she goes.

**If you enjoyed this excerpt,
read *His Lost Love* now!**

ALSO BY AVA RYAN

Fairy Tale Billionaires Series
The Billionaire's Princess
The Billionaire's Beauty
The Billionaire's Cinderella

Manhattan Billionaires
His Lost Love

To DH
XOXO

ACKNOWLEDGMENTS

Once again, special thanks to Nina Grinstead and the team at Grey's Promotions for helping me launch this book and to Croco Designs for the lovely covers. And huge thanks to my writer's brain trust of friends. Love you!

Excerpt from *His Lost Love* © 2020 by Ava Ryan

ABOUT THE AUTHOR

Ava Ryan is an author of sexy contemporary romance. Her favorite things, in no special order, are animals, her family, cookies, people with great senses of humor and love stories. Currently in her writer's cave (ostensibly working hard on her next book while also checking Netflix every few hours to make sure she hasn't missed a new true crime documentary show), she loves hearing from readers via her website or social media.

If you love billionaire alpha males, the feisty women who snag their hearts and books that end with a happily ever after, you've come to the right place.

Please make sure to Subscribe to Ava's VIP List to stay in the loop about her latest releases and upcoming books.

Finally, don't forget to follow her on Amazon and/or BookBub to learn about any special promotions on her books.